From Stockport With Love

SCEPTRE

Also by David Bowker

The Death Prayer
The Secret Sexist
The Butcher of Glastonbury

From Stockport With Love

David Bowker

SCEPTRE

First published in 1999 by Hodder and Stoughton
A division of Hodder Headline PLC
A Sceptre Book

10 9 8 7 6 5 4 3 2 1

British Library C.I.P.
A CIP catalogue record for this title is available
from the British Library.

ISBN 0 340 73853 7

Typeset by Palimpsest Book Production Limited,
Polmont, Stirlingshire

Printed and bound in Great Britain by
Mackays of Chatham PLC, Chatham, Kent

Hodder and Stoughton
A division of Hodder Headline PLC
338 Euston Road
London NW1 3BH

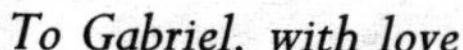

To Gabriel, with love

ACKNOWLEDGMENTS

I could not have written this book without Ian Lancaster Fleming, a truly gifted author who was capable of producing great literature. Thank God he never bothered. Without James Bond, the world would be a very dull place indeed.

Love and thanks to my friend David Lancaster, for inspiring me to write *From Stockport With Love*.

A huge thank you to Barbara Broccoli, Michael G. Wilson and all at *Eon Productions* for continuing to make the only Bond films worthy of the name and to Peter Janson-Smith, Ian Fleming's literary executor, for permission to quote from *For Your Eyes Only*. Love to every actor that has played 007, all of whom have brought something unique to the role. N.B. John Bryce's views on Roger Moore are not shared by me, and they are *certainly* not shared by my girlfriend.

Closer to home, a golden bullet to special agent Robert Kirby for his work in and out of the field. Love to Jessica Buckman, the finest Moneypenny a spy could wish for. For his invaluable help with this book, my Editor Neil Taylor has earned my gratitude and respect. I'm also indebted to my copy-Editor, Myrna Blumberg, for her wisdom and her Chardonnay. Also: a SPECTRE island-sized 'thank you' to Paul Mendelson for his advice on gambling.

I owe Vodka Martinis (shaken, not stirred) to Raymond Benson for his excellent book THE JAMES BOND BEDSIDE COMPANION and to Steven Jay Rubin for his equally accomplished COMPLETE JAMES BOND MOVIE ENCYCLOPEDIA. Both volumes saved me a great deal of time.

Lastly, I'd like to send my special love to Jane, my son and all the staff at Great Ormond Street Hospital.

'M looked sharply at Bond. "How's your coefficient of toughness, James?"

'. . . Bond didn't like personal questions. He didn't know what to answer, nor what the truth was. He had not got a wife or children – had never suffered the tragedy of a personal loss. He had not had to stand up to blindness or a mortal disease. He had absolutely no idea how he would face these things that needed so much more toughness than he had ever had to show . . .'

Ian Fleming, *For Your Eyes Only*

1

Diapers Are Forever

I went to see *Goldeneye* on the night before the baby was born. Tracy stayed at home, not because she was nine months' pregnant but because she thought Bond films were boring and infantile. I hadn't been to watch a Bond film at the cinema since 1977, when I saw *The Spy Who Loved Me* and decided enough was enough.

Throughout my childhood and early teens, I'd been a James Bond fanatic. Then I discovered politics and drugs and concluded that it wasn't cool to like books or films about a man who killed people on behalf of the British Establishment.

Because I was now thirty-seven, and no longer gave a shit whether people thought I was cool or not, I went to see *Goldeneye*. The cinema audience cheered and laughed in all the right places, but I didn't have a good time. I spent the entire film missing my dad and Sean Connery, in that order.

But any Bond film, with or without Sean, was a definite improvement on reality. When I emerged from the cinema,

I felt exactly what I'd felt as a boy; that the world did not measure up to my Bondian dreams. Where was my Aston Martin? Where were the girls in bikinis, famous for one film only? Where was my Walther PPK, my hairy chest, my spear gun, my theme tune, my licence to kill? Where was my life?

As the deserted District Line train that carried me home rattled and swayed through the dark, and the piss-poor but annoyingly catchy theme song to *Goldeneye* kept plodding through my head, I wondered if my father felt the same sense of controlled panic when I was about to be born. Or did he simply ache to hold me in his rough, sinewy arms, arms that smelt of printing ink, Old Spice and tobacco? Yes, I thought. That's exactly how it was. Dad was mad about babies, other people's as well as his own. Dad felt what fathers are supposed to feel.

All I felt was a growing sense of unease.

Hoping for reassurance, I'd asked various fathers of my acquaintance what it meant to have a newborn baby in the house. They responded with comments like: 'It means you've got a newborn baby in the house' or 'It means you'll be up to your neck in shit, piss and sick.' Being men, and therefore dedicated to the pursuit of oafishness in all its forms, regardless of their respective levels of intelligence or sensitivity, none of them said anything remotely helpful. Under normal circumstances, I would have asked my dad. But he had recently suffered a near-lethal stroke, and all he could say now was: 'Are you, are you.'

These two words had no meaning, they were simply the

only remnants of polite conversation remaining to him and he repeated them endlessly to anyone who chanced to be listening, perhaps hoping to divert their attention from the desperate hopelessness of his condition.

Of course, I could have easily tricked a conversation out of Dad.

ME: 'I'm going to be a father.'

DAD: 'Are you?'

ME: 'But I'm assailed by feelings of doubt.'

DAD: 'Ah.'

ME: 'I don't know what a father does. Who can teach me?'

DAD: 'You.'

ME: 'Really? You think I'm capable of taking care of a helpless infant?'

DAD: 'You are.'

ME: 'Thanks, Dad. I honestly don't know what I'd have done without you.'

But what if the manufactured conversation hadn't gone according to plan?

ME: 'Dad, I'm going to be a father.'

DAD: 'Aghhhh! You?'

ME: 'Yes. It's not that difficult, after all. I mean, I am having sex with a woman.

DAD (*incredulous*): 'You? Are you?'

The baby had been Tracy's idea. She'd spent the last two years sighing at the sight of small children. She loved all babies, including the square-headed ones with startled eyes and ears like dinner plates. I hadn't shared her ardent desire for parenthood. Nor had I planned to die childless. I was sure that I'd start a family one day; the same day that I made an honest tax return and threw away my modest collection of pornographic magazines.

But faced with the prospect of watching the person I loved more than anything in the world withering from the womb outwards, I capitulated. Tracy and I made a pact. We would make a baby. When that baby was born, Tracy would give up work and become a full-time mother. Because I earned more money than my wife, I would support all three of us until a better idea came along. During the day, I would work in my study as before and Tracy would do her best to protect me from my offspring and its strange, unholy cravings.

But as the months passed and Tracy fell more and more in love with the stranger sleeping in her belly, I started to experience a mounting sense of foreboding. I began to stare at the calendar, willing time to flow backwards. My fears were partly trivial. I'd led a fairly selfish life and wasn't looking forward to being kept awake all night. But it was more than that. I couldn't stop thinking that something was wrong, that my child might be born dead or with parts missing.

The ultrasound scans and blood tests had revealed no abnormalities. But my dark presentiments wouldn't go away. I couldn't confide in Tracy, because she had ludicrous faith in my judgement, practically treating me like an Oracle. When someone we knew became seriously ill, Tracy often asked me if they were going to live or die. ('How the hell should I know?' I'd protest. 'Because you *know things*,' she'd always say.)

Tracy was my best friend, my all-time favourite human being. All of her energies were concentrated on the person inside her and its imminent entry into the world. She was happy, perhaps happier than she'd ever been. She didn't need or deserve my auguries of doom. So I said nothing.

Like James Bond, we lived in a Chelsea flat, in a quiet square, although several malicious acquaintances, including our postman, had tried to insinuate that we actually lived in Fulham. When I got home, all the lights were on. I didn't think there was anything odd about this. Tracy hated the dark and often left lights on needlessly. But when she staggered down the hall with her coat on, weeping and cheering at the same time, I realised that something momentous had happened.

'Oh, where've you been?' she whispered, throwing her arms around me. 'I've been crying my eyes out.'

'What's wrong?'

'I think my waters have broken.'

'You "think"? Don't you know?'

She laughed. 'Well, either that or I keep pissing myself.'

We walked into the kitchen. Robotically, I filled the kettle with water and switched it on. 'Is that why you're crying?'

'Is it hell. It was 'cos you weren't here, you big divvy. I was scared of having the baby without you.'

Tracy's face suddenly came sharply into focus. I realised I hadn't really looked at my wife for months, too tense and preoccupied to see how lovely she was. She was a small, darkly pretty woman of thirty with wide cheekbones and shockingly green eyes. Pregnancy had swelled Tracy and her eyes to preposterous proportions.

At school, she had invariably been picked to play the Virgin Mary in Nativity plays. It was easy to see why. Tracy had always looked sensible and maternal, even as a child. She radiated sweetness and warmth, love without lust, which was why homeless beggars and nice old men on buses liked to flirt with her. They could tell on sight that as long as they behaved themselves, she'd laugh at their jokes and never tell them to fuck off.

Her parents were from Dublin, but the family had moved to North London when she was nine. Tracy only thought of herself as Irish when she was listening to Sinead O'Connor or watching the Irish football team losing valiantly to a superior side. I only thought of her as Irish on those not infrequent occasions when she turned to me, in the middle of a calm and civil discussion, to tell me I was talking a load of fucking bollocks.

Before the kettle had boiled, I started to get jumpy. 'Shit. I'm not doing anything. What should I be doing?'

Tracy explained that all I needed to do was pack my toothbrush and some clothes. She'd already phoned the hospital and been advised to go there immediately. Without the protection of the amniotic fluid, the baby was highly vulnerable to infection.

So my wife had packed a bag, called a taxi and written me a frantic explanatory note that she'd left on the kitchen table. ('John, this is awful but I'm in labour and I've gone to the hospital. Please come as soon as you can. I love you more than you'll ever know, Tracy.')

These scrawled lines brought a lump to my throat. They reminded me of the Valentine message in *The Guardian* that had brought us together. I'd just moved to London when I met my future wife at Bill's Advertising Agency, the agency that I still work for. She was a visualiser, a job description that brings to mind William Blake, seeing angels in trees on Hampstead Heath. In fact, her role at the agency involved nothing more ethereal than refining Bill's loathsomely limited ideas.

Bill was the managing director of the agency. He was no William Blake. He'd say something like: 'I see girls, I see long hair, I see pert little tits,' and Tracy would go away and sketch three mermaids in a swimming pool. I loved Tracy on sight, but felt sure that she was indifferent to me, until the morning she caught me reading *The Mirror* and advised me, quite strictly, to go out and buy *The Guardian* at once.

I took her advice. It was 14 February 1985. *The Guardian* was full of Valentine messages that its wet liberal readers had sent to each other. I was suddenly intrigued. Had Tracy been trying to tell me something? Excitedly, I ploughed through pages of short, witless Valentines, all along the lines of 'TIGGY BEAR, Mummy Furry Toes wants to share your hunny' until I came to the communique that could only have come from her. It read:

> **JB, you don't know it,**
> **but you are much loved.**

This sentence gave me the courage to tell Tracy that I adored her. I shortly discovered that she hadn't placed the Valentine, didn't even fancy me much, but at least liked me enough to accept a dinner invitation. So all that followed, from our blossoming love to the wedding and the small interloper in her belly; all of these things were directly attributable to my extraordinary capacity for self-deception.

On our arrival at the Chelsea and Westminster Hospital, we were placed in a small side-ward while we waited for Tracy to go into labour. Tracy thought she was already in labour but the midwife who examined her informed us that my wife was not experiencing fully fledged contractions, only half-arsed contractions known as 'tightenings'.

'Oh, fucking hell,' moaned Tracy as soon as we were alone. We were lying side-by-side on a ridiculously narrow bed. Tracy had tears in her eyes. 'John, I don't think I'm going to be able to stand this.'

''Course you are,' I said automatically.

'How do you know? I'm in agony and I haven't even had a proper contraction yet. Stop talking through your arse.'

'I can't help it. That's where my vocal chords are situated. And why are you getting so mad at me?'

'Sorry.' Her face crumpled up in pain. 'Ow! Ow!' Through her tears she said, a little grudgingly: 'I love you, I suppose.'

Her pain subsided momentarily. I started to notice the room, with its fly-spattered drapes, the worn and shiny linoleum, and that universal hospital aroma of old urine. Tracy said: 'Do you think they'd give me a Caesarean? If I asked nicely?'

'No,' I said. 'You don't want a Caesarean.'

'Yes I do.'

'You'll never be able to wear a bikini again.'

'I hate bikinis.'

'Tracy, forget it. They're only going to give you a Caesarean if you or the baby are in trouble.'

Her bottom lip began to quiver. 'I *am* in trouble,' she whimpered.

'OK.' I soothed. 'I'll get a nurse. Shall I? Shall I ring for a nurse?'

'They're called midwives.'

'A midwife, then. Do you want me to get one?'

'No. No.' She rolled over onto her side as another little dagger sliced through her abdomen. 'Yes! Yes!'

On the wall there was a button with a small diagram of a nurse on its surface. Fifty seconds later, our midwife strolled in, a friendly but slightly bolshy Welsh girl called Sian. I was disappointed. She didn't look remotely like the woman in the diagram.

'What's the matter?' said Sian.

'Take a wild guess,' I said. (Tracy was rolling about on the bed, holding her belly and weeping.)

'C'mon lovie,' said Sian, lifting up Tracy's night dress in a rather familiar way. 'Let's have a look at you.'

After subjecting Tracy to a detailed manual examination, Sian confessed to finding nothing wrong. She sat on the end of the bed and regarded us both calmly. 'OK. Maybe now would be a good time to discuss your birth plan.'

'Ow! Ow! Jesus!' said Tracy.

I said: 'Tracy wants a natural birth, free from medication or any kind of surgical intervention.'

Sian was sceptical. 'Is that true, Tracy?'

Tracy shook her head vigorously.

Sian sternly advised that Tracy should scrap her birth plan and accept all the pain relief that the hospital could offer. Eagerly, Tracy agreed.

At 3 a.m., when the real labour pains started, Tracy was given gas and air. She giggled inanely for a few minutes, then started to scream. One pethidine injection and five hours later, her cervix was only five centimetres dilated and she desperately needed the lavatory.

'Would you mind taking her?' asked Sian. 'The woman in the next cubicle needs watching, see. She's having a difficult birth.'

'Well, what do you think Tracy's having?' I demanded.

'A poo, by the sound of it.'

I got Tracy to the WC in the nick of time. She sat there, laughing, crying and farting, covering her face in shame.

With my arms folded I said: 'So *this* is what you get up to when you go to the bathroom.'

'I don't believe it,' she groaned drunkenly. 'You've seen me shitting.'

I considered referring to the passage in *Lady Chatterley's Lover* where the gamekeeper tells Constance Chatterley that he could never love 'a woman as couldna piss nor shit'. But it seemed a ridiculous time to resort to quotations, so I just said: 'Tracy, so what? I love you,' and passed her the toilet roll.

A few moments later she said: 'Oh, God, no! Now you've seen me wiping my bum!'

'Would you rather I wiped it?'

She warded me away with her free hand. 'No! No!'

We returned to the side-ward and Tracy continued to weep in pain. It was terrible to watch her suffer. I had never felt so impotent in my life. With *Goldeneye* so fresh in my mind, it occurred to me that it was high time that 'Q', played by the lovely Desmond Llewellyn, walked through the door to say: 'Pay attention, 007. This may look like an ordinary typewriter. In fact, it's a CPR: a Computerised Pain Relocater. Simply tap in the name of anybody you really dislike and they'll feel your wife's labour pains while she feels little more than a mild discomfort in the genital area.'

If only.

By 7 a.m., Tracy was screaming so loudly that they gave her an epidural. As soon as the anaesthetic took effect, Tracy did what I'd been yearning to do all night. She fell asleep.

All I could do now was wait. I went to the Gents and studied myself in the mirror. It was worse than I'd feared. My hair was sticking up stupidly in several places, my eyes were red and bloodshot and my face was the colour of cold porridge. 'You unconfident-looking bastard,' I said to myself accusingly.

I left the hospital and visited the Häagen Dazs shop across the road for a cup of strong coffee to take out. Then I returned to the maternity wing and found a grubby sitting room with a NO SMOKING sign above the door and cigarette burns in the arms and cushions of its antique chairs. The rickety bookcase under the window contained all the usual fare; tattered and grease-stained paperbacks by Wilbur Smith, Maeve Binchy and Danielle Steele, a Book Club edition of a Prince Charles biography. To my delight, there were also three Ian Fleming paperbacks: *From Russia With Love*, *On Her Majesty's Secret Service* and *Goldfinger*.

I felt the warm inner thrill of a lost love rediscovered as I picked up *From Russia With Love*. To hell with *Goldeneye*. This was the real thing. I recognised the paperback's faded cover: a Fabergé egg against a blood-red background. The elderly brownish-yellow pages smelled of holidays long ago, of cigarettes and Ambre Solaire, sand, sunlight and dust.

I'd thrown all my Bond novels away when I was a student, afraid that girls would see them on my bookshelf and mistake me for the person that I actually was. I first read *From Russia With Love* when I was ten, mostly during school lunch-breaks. I still remember feeling disturbed and excited by the sadism of the fight between the two gypsy girls, and startled when Rosa Klebb's breasts were likened to a 'badly-packed sandbag'. Startled because I completely misread the phrase and thought Fleming had written 'badly-packed sandwich'.

I put the book down, plucked *Goldfinger* off the shelf. The sleeve was spanned by a gold-painted woman, lying face-down, her golden bottom obscured by a clumsy insert of Sean Connery in a tuxedo. 'BOND'S BACK IN ACTION!' vaunted the blurb. I was reminded of a sentence from the movie poster for *From Russia With Love*: 'His New Incredible Women, His New Incredible Adventures' and realised that such terrible slogans had probably propelled me with the force of a jet-pack into my laughable profession. (I'm an advertising copy-writer.)

I sank into one of the fag-scarred armchairs with *On Her Majesty's Secret Service*. The cover featured a bright expanse of snow onto which a wedding ring and some drops of blood had fallen. Most of Bond's women possessed 'taut' breasts, or breasts that 'tautened with desire' when Bond was in the immediate vicinity.

I couldn't remember whether Teresa di Vicenzo, the heroine of this novel had such a chest. I turned to the love scene in Chapter 4, but found no tautness to speak of. All Bond does is place his hand over the 'little hill that was her left breast'. This line would have been more than enough, however, to have given me a tautness in my shorts when I first read this scene.

I smiled in affectionate recognition at the familiar and highly distinctive Fleming vocabulary. Words that I had once looked up in a dictionary and slavishly committed to memory. Imperious, impassive, indifferent, inimical, ironical. Quizzical. Non-committal, nondescript, equable, deferential, taciturn, ruthless. Meticulous. Perfunctory, abrupt, brusque, blunt, curt, cursory. Curious. Stolid, staunch, stoical. Sensual.

Then there were the short, *brusque* sentences: 'James Bond lit another cigarette and inhaled thoughtfully. This was going to be a tough assignment. A case of kill or be killed. Someone was going to die. Bond smiled – a hard, cruel smile. Better make damned sure it wasn't him.'

Or Fleming's peculiarly dogmatic assertions about food, wine, and foreigners. For instance, when ordering caviare in a restaurant, one 'never seems to get enough toast with it'. ('Oh, Ian! You mean you've noticed that too?') Taittinger Blanc de Blanc Brut '43 is probably the finest champagne in the world. Good Texans are probably the finest people in the world.

And what about the sentences ending in question marks? The questions that Bond asked himself? Did they add anything to the prose? Or were they just a device to fill up the empty pages?

Perhaps they were like all the exclamation marks! Proof that Fleming wrote these novels a long time ago! I turned to Chapter 17! And counted eight exclamation marks in a single paragraph! Hell! Fleming always overdid the exclamation marks! Particularly during the action scenes!

Yes, in the light of experience, it was easy to belittle Fleming's work. But when I was young, these books weren't merely sexy adventure stories. They were instructional manuals that taught me how to think and behave; to dress, eat, drink and kill. To read about Bond was never enough. I wanted to *be* him.

My disappointment and incredulity would have been boundless had I realised that Fleming had based 007 on himself. As a boy, I never really liked the look of Ian Lancaster Fleming – not as he appeared in the photographs on the back of the Bond paperbacks. He always looked like some sour, ageing libertine who'd just caught fire – an illusion created by the great cloud of cigarette smoke that was always drifting out of his sneering aristocratic mouth. He was too old, too unhealthy and frankly, too soppy-looking to be James Bond.

The hero I envisaged as I devoured Fleming's novels always looked like Sean Connery, probably because I saw *Thunderball* before reading any of Fleming's books. Too young to view the early 007 films the first time round, I caught up with *Dr No*, *From Russia With Love* and *Goldfinger* in the seventies, when they were re-released on James Bond cinema double-bills.

I can still vividly recall my disappointment when I went to the Gents at the cinema in the interval and looked at myself in the mirror, expecting to see Sean's ruggedly handsome face smirking back at me. Instead, I saw a sensitive, fat-faced schoolboy who had never had sex or shot a bit-part actor in the line of duty. A boy who only a partially sighted lunatic could possibly have mistaken for agent 007.

I gulped down my coffee, then laughed aloud at the memory of my early Bondian pretensions: calling out 'Suivi!' during a game of Snap with my brother, or trying out Connery's one-liners on a sexy posh girl I met on the beach on holiday. ('Do you know anything about shells?' she asked me. 'No,' I replied, 'but I know a little about women.')

I turned to the last page of *OHMSS*, read the bit where Bond's wife is shot dead soon after their wedding, and Bond cradles her head in his lap and tells the police patrolman that he and Tracy have 'all the time in the world'. I recalled the painful lump in my throat when I saw this scene, faithfully reproduced, on the big screen at the Davenport Cinema. My dad was sitting beside me.

Dad.

His name was Myles Bryce. My mother, feeling that Myles was too showy a name for everyday use, had always called him ‘M’. As a boy, it thrilled me that my unglamorous working-class father had the same title as the Head of the British Secret Service.

But this was nothing to the thrill I received when I first picked up *Live And Let Die* and discovered that while he was in America on the trail of Mr Big, Bond called himself *John Bryce*. At that age – I must have been about fourteen – I hadn’t heard of Carl Gustav Jung or Synchronicity, the term Jung applied to meaningful coincidence. I simply felt that if James Bond was John Bryce, then it was fair to assume that John Bryce was James Bond.

Tracy remained unconscious for six hours. When she awoke, girlishly excited and utterly refreshed, her cervix had fully dilated and the baby’s head was emerging into the birth canal. The effects of the epidural were wearing off, so that Tracy was now able to push the child out.

It was an easy delivery, with very little tearing or bleeding. I forgot all my doubts and fears and watched in rapt amazement as Sian the midwife hauled the baby out and laid it over Tracy’s warm belly. We had a son. He was dark haired and perfect, with long, strong limbs.

‘Oh darling, darling,’ said Tracy, stroking the baby’s damp head, moved to tears by the love she already felt for him.

We waited for the baby to cry. Instead, he lay still, opening and closing his mouth like a drowning fish. Working quickly, Sian sucked mucus from his mouth and throat with a length of plastic tubing. The baby continued to gasp. I broke into a hot sweat. Was this why I’d been dreading the birth? Was our child destined to die before we'd had the chance to hold him?

There was a red emergency button on the wall. Sian pressed it. Then she wrapped the baby in a green sheet.

'What's the matter?' asked Tracy, getting scared. 'He's all right, isn't he?'

'He's fine,' answered Sian. 'He's just a little flat.'

'Flat?' I echoed.

'Oh, it just means that he's been born a bit out of breath. It often happens after a long labour. The baby gets exhausted.' She patted my son's hand gently. 'Almost as tired as Mummy, aren't we, darling?'

A paediatrician rushed in and started to massage the baby's chest. Then, frowning to himself, he picked up my son and hurried out of the room with him.

Mystified, Tracy said: 'Where've they gone?'

'Special care,' said Sian.

'John, go with him,' instructed Tracy.

I caught up with the paediatrician in the corridor outside. He frowned when he saw me, as if my face was familiar but he couldn't quite place me.

'What's happening?' I demanded.

The paediatrician was small, harassed and not noticeably friendly. Without looking at me, he said: 'I'm putting him in the special care unit. No cause for concern. Just a precaution.'

We entered a clean, bright room that contained about six incubators. The paediatrician laid the baby in the only vacant incubator and a grey-haired senior staff nurse rushed over to lend a hand. Like her colleague, the nurse barely glanced at me. I felt the powerful urge to push them both out of the way. I couldn't understand why they weren't consulting me or justifying their actions.

'I'd love to know what's going on,' I said, my irritation showing.

'I'm sorry,' said the nurse in a voice that meant she was nothing of the kind. 'We're rushed off our feet.' As if she thought she was doing me a colossal favour, she passed me a hissing oxygen tube. 'Here. Hold this underneath his nose.'

I complied, while the doctor and nurse attempted to insert a drip into the baby's hand. They kept failing to find a vein, and the baby made things harder for them by knocking their hands away with his flailing arms. Good boy! Give the bastards hell.

When my son was fully plugged and wired, his head under a perspex oxygen box, and I was still brooding over the way I'd been treated, a young student nurse asked me if I'd like a cup of tea. I said yes. Shortly, she returned with the tea and a small plate of plain biscuits. I thanked her profusely, grateful to be acknowledged.

'No prob,' she said, winking at me.

A machine above the baby's incubator began to bleep urgently. Nonchalantly, the student nurse stabbed a button with her forefinger. The machine went silent.

'You know,' she said seriously, looking down at my son. 'I don't think I've ever seen a nicer baby.'

Not knowing what to say, I simply smiled. She smiled back. 'Have you got a name for him yet?'

'Yes,' I said, thinking suddenly of the man who had played such a vital role in my life. 'There's only one possible name for him. We're going to call him James.'

2

Interview With M

Tracy worshipped James from the very beginning. Not from the beginning of his life, or the moment of his conception, or even the time she first longed for motherhood. Tracy worshipped James from the beginning of her own life.

On the evening after his birth, I went home to get some sleep. Tracy stayed in the hospital with James. Before going to bed, I gazed at the photograph that I keep on the wall of my study. It's a portrait of Tracy, aged three, clutching a plastic mouse in her small fat hands and looking up at the camera with huge, doleful eyes.

When female children enter the world, all the eggs that they'll ever need are stored in their ovaries. So when this picture of Tracy was taken, the egg that eventually became James was sitting inside her. And Tracy's three-year-old eyes were already dark with all the fear, the pride and the tenderness that she would one day feel for him.

So as far as parental love was concerned, my wife had quite a head start on me. During those first few days of my son's life, I waited to feel the sudden gush of irresistible warmth that meant I was falling in love with him. But nothing happened. He remained remote from me, as lovely and unknowable as a distant star.

My sense of alienation was compounded by the presence of Tracy's parents. Patrick, her father, looked slightly biblical: tall, with white flowing hair and a beard. I don't know what he was like as a builder, but as a father, he was a complete disaster. Neurotic and depressive, he was unable to hold the simplest conversation without revealing his awkwardness and peculiar lack of interest in anything but himself. To call Patrick Duggan socially inept would be like describing Pol Pot as slightly less than benign.

Mostly, Patrick was silent. His good moods were rare, but when they arrived he would ask rash questions like: 'How are you?' or 'What have you been doing with y'self?' Any reply that exceeded two syllables in length would cause him to look away, his eyes glazed over with boredom. When Patrick asked a question, therefore, the most sensible response would be to say: 'Fuck off.' Better to insult him while you still had his attention.

I had never told him to fuck off, because I loved my wife and did not wish to make her already strained relations with her parents any worse. At least he was easy to ignore. Although eager to visit his new grandson, he was invariably more eager to leave. When he first saw James in the special care unit, he smiled, said: 'Ah, so that's the little fella, is it?' then immediately went outside to sit in the corridor, reading the paper.

Florence, Tracy's mum, was more difficult to get rid of. In her youth, she had been, in her own words, 'a real Irish beauty'. Nowadays, she resembled Kim Hunter as the female chimpanzee in *Planet Of The Apes*. While Tracy and the baby were in hospital, Florence arrived early in the morning and left late at night, never taking the hint when Tracy and I wanted to be alone, always behaving as if the baby was a private matter between Tracy and herself, not really my business at all.

On the second night of James's life, when Patrick had gone home to sulk and Florence was still hovering by Tracy's bed, I said: 'Actually Florence, it's rather late . . . would it be OK if me and Tracy had a bit of time on our own?'

Her reaction was encouraging. 'Yes, of course. I understand. You need your own space.'

We thought this meant that she was finally going home. Instead, she walked over to a vacant bed on the opposite side of the ward and sat down, watching us forlornly, while we held hands and whispered about what a silly cow she was.

Every time Florence saw James, she recited the same speech: 'Doesn't he look like Tracy? And although you never met him, John, he has a look of my father. The same mouth and chin.'

To which Tracy would say: 'I think he looks like John.'

This would be Florence's cue to observe a two-minute silence.

Tracy's sisters, Siobhan and Katrin, reacted normally to the baby, having no problem with the concept that he might possess one or two of his father's genes.

Patrick and Florence always behaved as if I had misappropriated their daughter rather than married her. They only left messages on our answering machine for Tracy ('Just ringing to see how you are, darling'). If I answered the door or the phone to them, they were civil, but only in the way one would be civil to a stranger.

Naively, I had expected the baby's arrival to change all that. His very existence was living proof that Tracy's genes had officially merged with my own. Whatever was hers was now mine, and vice versa. Florence, however, preferred to regard the child as the result of a miraculous collaboration between Tracy, herself and the virgin Mary.

In her more tolerant moments, Tracy tried to tell me that Florence's behaviour owed a great deal to Patrick. 'You've got to feel sorry for her. She doesn't understand that a man and wife need to be alone, because she's never wanted to be alone with Dad. She hasn't got the faintest idea what a normal relationship is like.' When Tracy was tired, she simply said: 'She's a stupid old bag, I hate her.'

Most of the time, Tracy's feelings for her mother were an amalgam of these two extremes: she despaired of Florence, but felt sorry for her. Yet childbirth had exhausted my wife. She lacked the energy to put her mother right. That grim task fell to me. I probably handled it badly. I took Tracy's mother for a cup of tea in the hospital canteen and said: 'Florence, when we get home, Tracy and I want to be alone for a while.'

She started nodding before I'd finished speaking. 'Of course you do. You *need your space*.'

'No. We need a few weeks. Months, maybe. To get used to the baby.'

Florence looked glum. 'But you will need help?'

I smiled at her. It was a cold, ruthless smile. 'Florence, if we need help, you'll be the first to know . . .'

But when we took James home, I was unable to feel any closer to him. If anything, I felt further away. Without Florence to use as a scapegoat, I was forced to face the true source of my resentment. I had become a father. I didn't want to be a father. Tracy had ruined my life. But I had been her willing accomplice. When she had become pregnant with James after one afternoon of 'trying', I had even boasted about how marvellously fertile I was. What the hell had possessed me?

'Help me bath him, John,' Tracy would urge me. 'It's fun. Why don't you help me?'

'I don't want to.'

Then, to the baby: 'Oh, what a grumpy daddy. Grumpy, grumpy!'

It wasn't that I disliked my son, or resented him for behaving like a baby. Quite the reverse. He didn't cry that often. He was placid and attractive. Looking at the situation objectively, I could see that we'd been blessed with a spectacular child. But inwardly, I felt that I had once been free, but would never be free again. It was impossible to see how a person so small could take over an entire flat.

When James was five days old, I felt so desperate that I rang my brother.

'I was going to ring you,' he said defensively. 'I was planning on coming over next week.'

'Can't you come today? I want to talk to you.'

Richard was eighteen months younger than me and about one hundred thousand pounds richer. He was tall and funny and not much use in a knife fight. Richard was a chartered accountant, which apparently isn't the same as an accountant. For reasons that he had never explained to my satisfaction, this meant my brother couldn't balance my books or tell me how to avoid paying income tax.

By making this pilgrimage to our Chelsea flat in Fulham, Richard wasn't exactly putting himself out. He only lived in Barnes. But as usual, he arrived laden with gifts, witty and warm, making it impossible for us to condemn his tardiness. When he saw James, Richard was visibly shocked.

'God,' he said, his eyes filling with tears. 'He's gorgeous.'

Tracy was thrilled by his reaction. 'He is, isn't he? Do you want to hold him?'

Richard gratefully accepted her offer, then practically danced around the room with James, reminding me for all the world of my father. During the dance, he supplied James with useful football tips. 'Now, don't forget, you and me support Man United. We don't like Leeds and we loathe, detest and absolutely hate Liverpool FC.'

We ordered a Chinese takeaway. When the food arrived, Richard paid. He liked to pay for things, partly because he had more money than us, partly because it was his way of apologising for hardly ever getting in touch. While we ate, Tracy fed James, his head in her left hand and a spring roll in her right.

'Good God,' said Richard, eyeing them reverently. 'I'm not just saying this. That is one bloody marvellous baby.'

Later, I walked my brother to the tube. Richard chatted happily about a woman from his office he was hoping to sleep with. I only half-listened. I couldn't stop wondering why my brother felt more for my son than I did. At the entrance to Fulham Broadway station, we passed two prostitutes, leaning against a wall. One of them said: 'How about it, love? You can come anywhere you like, as long as it's not in me hair.'

Tittering childishly about this charming invitation, we descended to the platform. While we stamped and shivered in the cold, Richard asked me what I'd wanted to talk to him about. But I no longer felt like telling him.

So I lied. 'It was about Dad, actually. I was wondering if you felt like going back with us when we show him his grandson.'

'Yeah! Great idea.'

'Really?'

'Yeah. Great. All of us together.' I heard the guilt in his voice. Richard, traditionally the good son, white hat to my black hat, had only been to visit Dad in hospital once. 'When are you going?'

'This weekend.'

Richard's face clouded over. 'Shit. I'm busy this weekend.'

'OK. How about next weekend?'

He shuffled uneasily. 'No. No. Better leave it.' With a swift nervous movement, he reached into his coat and produced a fat leather wallet. 'How are you fixed for money?'

'Not so good,' I admitted.

Decisively, he flicked open the wallet and handed me five twenty-pound notes. 'Here. Take it.'

'Are you sure?'

He nodded confidently. 'Put it towards your trip to Stockport.'

The train was pulling into the station. My brother snorted in amusement. 'It's unreal. My brother's a daddy.'

'My brother's an uncle.'

The news came as a shock to him. 'Christ! I am, aren't I? We're almost related!'

The train stopped. Its doors hissed open. Richard slapped me on the arm. 'I've had a great time.' The train was virtually empty. He climbed aboard and lingered by the open doors. 'I might even come again.'

'Make it soon,' I urged.

Richard started to smirk. 'I'll come when I want to . . .'

'As long as it isn't in my hair,' I rejoined.

We sniggered in unison. The doors closed and the train moved off. Richard stopped laughing and sat down, looking awkward and vulnerable. I waved to him but he didn't see me.

Richard and I were raised in a modest semi-detached house in Hazel Grove near Stockport, with more space around it than any contemporary architect could possibly allow. Because our family home was situated on a corner, it boasted a front garden, a back garden and a long sweeping lawn at the side.

Yet as a child, I was ashamed of this house and the meagre income that went with it, ashamed because I wanted to be like

James Bond and couldn't imagine Sean Connery living in such a dump. What I failed to appreciate was that Thomas Sean Connery was born and raised in an Edinburgh slum, that as a baby he slept in the bottom drawer of his parents' wardrobe because they couldn't afford a cot for him, and that if young Tommy Connery had moved into my neighbourhood, he would have considered himself to be a very lucky bastard indeed.

On the last weekend in January, I took my son back to this house, the house I was born in. The taxi cab parked on the corner, next to the sign that read Compton Drive. The grey-haired driver grunted and wheezed as he hauled our bags out of his boot and onto the pavement. Tracy carried James down the garden path while I fished in my pocket for money. The fare was five pounds fifty. I gave the driver six pounds and told him to keep the change. My largesse surprised and delighted him, reminding me that we were in the North of England. A London cabby would have told me where to shove a fifty-pence tip.

Tracy was waiting for me on the doorstep. The house was unlocked but no one was home. Tracy waited on the living-room sofa with the baby on her lap while I went in search of my mother. I found her in the garage, sitting at the wheel of Dad's Nissan Bluebird.

Although she couldn't drive and no one would have given her a licence in a million years, Mum had started the car and was revving the engine mercilessly. Since Dad's stroke, this had become a daily ritual for her. She'd go down to the garage in her apron and slippers, turn the ignition key, grip the steering wheel and jam her right foot down on the accelerator until black fumes poured copiously out of the exhaust.

Both my brother and I had tried to explain that as well as serving no useful purpose, this practice was guaranteed to flatten the car's battery, but Mum insisted that she was: 'Keeping the engine ticking over for M when he comes out of hospital.'

I rapped on the driver's window. My mother almost leapt through the roof. Holding her heart, she said: 'Oh, you silly bugger! You nearly frightened me to death.'

'Sorry.'

She switched off the engine, got out of the car and gave me a cursory hug. 'Where the devil have you been, lad? I've been worried sick.'

'Why?'

'You said you'd be here at quarter past eleven. When it got to half-past, and I still hadn't heard anything, I thought something terrible had happened. So I rang you up, but you didn't answer.'

'That's because we were in a tax . . .'

Before I could complete my sentence, my mother quitted my presence and trotted up the path to the house. She'd been waiting to meet her new grandson for the past week and was not about to let social niceties stand in her way. Tracy met her at the door, holding James. Mum's eyes went moist at the sight of him. 'Oh, M,' she said, snatching the baby out of Tracy's arms. 'He's the image of my M.'

Tracy agreed enthusiastically. I couldn't see any immediate resemblance, beyond the fact that they were both half-bald and had to wear nappies, but kept this depressing observation to myself.

I made a pot of tea. Mum held the baby, bewitched and mesmerised by him, yet still finding time to comment on Tracy's appearance. 'You don't look very well, young lady. Are you getting enough sleep?'

Tracy smiled wanly. 'No. But that goes with the territory, doesn't it?'

Mum didn't know what Tracy was talking about. 'I don't know about territory. You look as if you could do with a week in bed. Are you anaemic? You could do with taking a course of iron tablets . . .'

We went into the living room to drink our tea. Mum sat James in her lap and studied him. 'Ooh, he even frowns like Myles.'

'Surely it's just that all babies look like old men?' I ventured.

'Your dad isn't old,' she said defensively. 'Seventy isn't old these days.'

'Well, it isn't young.' I should have shut up then, while I had the chance. Instead, I added: 'Anyway, Dad thinks he's old.'

This was true. Shortly before his stroke, during one of our rare moments of privacy, M told me he had been feeling his age. For a man who had never admitted to being ill and seemed to regard going to bed with 'flu as evidence of homosexuality, this amounted to a confession of grave import. 'You don't look old,' I was able to answer honestly.

'I bloody feel it.' he replied grimly.

I recounted this conversation to Mum. 'All right,' she said. 'I don't want an argument.'

'Neither do I.'

'Well why are you arguing then?'

I was about to deny my part in any argument when Tracy silenced me with a warning nudge.

My mother's name is Ivy. She is a small, sturdy woman with a flat, combative face and short grey hair, cut mannishly and parted on the left. When she met my father she was a dancer – the kind of dancer who appeared in seaside shows at the end of the pier, grinning dementedly and kicking her legs at the audience in between the comedian and the man who did impressions of a train. The troupe she'd danced with had been famous in its day: The Sally Sherratt Showstoppers. Throughout my childhood, Mum's show business reminiscences had invariably been heralded by the magic words: 'When I was with Miss Sherratt'.

Mum adored Dad unequivocally, while holding him slightly responsible for luring her away from the glamour of the pier into a life of domestic servitude. She was deeply sentimental about Richard and Richard reciprocated.

But my relationship with Ivy had always been so dire that I had committed her past crimes to heart and hugged them to me like little jewels of poison, a bitter litany to recite whenever I needed someone to blame. As a child, I had nightmares in which my mother was Rosa Klebb. To be fair, Mum's slippers had never harboured steel spikes tipped in venom. But she had smacked me for nothing, given me no encouragement with my schoolwork, made my sweaters go all baggy by washing them at the wrong temperature. And what did she do that was worse, far worse than any of these things? She burned my copy of *Thunderball*.

My father and I didn't exactly get on like a house on fire either. He respected authority. I despised it in any form. He thought I was lazy because I slept till noon. He was probably right. But Dad was mentally lazy. If you gave him a book with a word like 'didactic' in it, he would sulk and put the book aside. He was undoubtedly intelligent, so his 'I-be-only-a-simple-peasant act' could be maddening.

Once, over dinner, I said to him: 'Dad, don't you think that unconsciously, on the deepest level, all human beings are linked?' 'No,' he answered flatly. 'I'm not clever enough to think things like that.' I explained that I wasn't clever enough either, that I'd borrowed this idea from the writings of Carl Gustav Jung. He gazed at me blankly for a few moments, then said: 'Aye, but at least you're clever enough to read Carl Whatever-his-name-is. I'm not.' With this, he returned his attention to his pork chop.

Yet I was never in any doubt that M wanted me to thrive, to flourish and excel. At school, I was a late developer. Dad stayed up with me, night after night, struggling to teach me to read and write. When he finally succeeded, I rewarded him by writing full-length comics and novels for his personal delectation.

Among these early masterpieces was a James Bond story called *To Guard A Living Target*, which demonstrates, with frightening clarity, how Ian Fleming had fucked me up for life: 'Finally, the Aston Martin skidded to a halt over Lovers' Leap. "Be Gentle," said Fiona, as Bond clambered over onto the back seat . . .'

Dad honoured me by not only pretending to read my juvenile drivel, but throwing in favourable reviews like 'Quite exciting' and 'I was nearly on the edge of my seat.' He went red in the face and hugged me every time I won a prize or passed an exam. 'Good lad,' he'd chuckle, ruffling my hair. 'Good lad.'

The phone rang. Mum turned pale and passed the baby to Tracy. Then she hurried down the hall. It was obvious what was going through her mind. She thought it was the hospital, ringing to say that Dad had taken a turn for the worse. We heard her snatch up the receiver and say: 'Yes?' in a breathless voice. Then, almost rudely: 'Oh, it's you Audrey. I thought it might have been the hospital . . . Yes, they've just this minute come through the door . . . He's lovely. Very bonny. No . . . actually, he's got a little look of our Richard . . .'

Tracy turned to me. 'Why do you always insist on winding your mother up?'

'I don't,' I responded feebly. 'She winds me up.'

'She's old. And she's got enough on her plate without you badgering her.'

'Lest we forget,' I said. 'We're talking about the woman who threw *Thunderball* on the fire.'

'I beg your pardon?'

'The first James Bond book I ever owned. My mum burned it.'

'When was this?'

'About 1969.'

Tracy started laughing. 'That recent? No wonder you're still upset.'

'It isn't funny.'

'John darling, I'm sorry, but it is a *bit* funny . . .'

When Mum returned, the baby needed changing. Mum stood over Tracy, criticising the mother through its child. After Tracy's recent plea for greater-tolerance-in-the-Ivy-department, I was gratified to see that she too was showing signs of irritation. 'Is Mummy drying all your little nooks and crannies, then? We don't want to get a nasty rash, do we?'

'Mum,' I said. 'Tracy's perfectly capable of changing a nappy.'

My mother turned to me and said: 'I bet you're not.'

Tracy flushed slightly as she said: 'Yes he is. John's a wonderful father.'

'Oh. Good,' said Mum, cowed by the sharpness of Tracy's response. 'I'm glad to hear it.'

A lump came to my throat. Tracy would have said anything to protect me. But she was lying through her teeth. I couldn't have changed a nappy to save my life.

While James cried and kicked his legs to create a diversion, I crept upstairs to my old bedroom and searched through the toy cars in the box at the bottom of the wardrobe. Among the scratched and mutilated Dinky toys I found a miniature steam roller that had belonged to my brother, and my old *Man From Uncle* car (press a button on the roof and the man in the passenger seat leans out of the window and shoots at the car in front). I still had one of my *Avengers* cars, too. Steed's Bentley had been lost or stolen, but Mrs Peel's Lotus Elan was more or less intact, although the miniature figure of Mrs Peel had gone AWOL, probably after some abortive adolescent attempt to have sex with her.

Yet none of these delights could hold a candle, or even a *Spectre Island* flame-thrower to my favourite souvenir of childhood: my James Bond Aston Martin DB5, especially designed for me by Corgi, the toy people.

Admittedly, the car was golden rather than silver – perhaps Corgi had been confused by the fact that the DB5 had featured in a film about a man who 'only loved gold' – and the figure at the wheel appeared to have a moustache, making him look more like my Uncle Bert than James Bond. Three of the tyres were missing and both the ejector seat and its hapless occupant were ejected onto some kid's lawn, long ago. But the twin machine guns under the headlamps still worked. I'm glad to say that the bulletproof shield for the rear window was also fully functional. Particularly useful for those days when the Man From Uncle is in the car behind.

I ran this precious memento of my boyhood up and down the window sill several times before I realised that Tracy was calling me. The taxi had arrived to take us to the hospital. I slipped the DB5 into neutral . . . I mean my pocket, went downstairs and dutifully bore the carry cot out to the cab. Mum and Tracy walked behind me. Mum was telling her how emotional M had become since his stroke.

'I'm just warning you,' she said. 'He's likely to cry when he sees the baby.'

'He never used to cry,' I said.

'No,' she admitted. I turned to look at Mum as I slid the carry cot onto the back seat of the car. She had aged and withered since Dad's stroke. But for a brief moment, she looked like a lovesick young girl. 'He didn't, did he?' she said, smiling wistfully. 'Funny, that. He never used to hold me hand either.' She laughed, half-proud, half-desolate. 'He can't get enough of me since his stroke.'

I went silent during the journey. I was thinking about my father. On the night M took me to see *Thunderball* I was about seven years old. As we drove into Davenport in our pale-blue Vauxhall Viva, I felt a mounting sense of excitement.

I'd already seen a television programme called *The Incredible World Of James Bond, 007*. I'd watched this with Dad, late one Saturday night. My mother had been out with 'the girls', whoever they were. My brother was in bed. It was just M and me. The programme featured clips from *Dr No*, *From Russia With Love* and *Goldfinger*, as well as a selection of scenes from the forthcoming *Thunderball*.

M seemed to enjoy the documentary as much as I did. During the commercial break, he toasted some crumpets. I remember biting into a crumpet as Bond unzipped Miss Taro's dress in a clip from *Dr No*. 'Take it slowly,' warned my dad. 'It could give you indigestion.' (Was he talking about the crumpet, or what 007 and Miss Taro were about to do next?)

After this initiation, there was to be no turning back. James Bond, like Blofeld in *OHMSS*, became 'something of a must for me'. One of my schoolfriends owned a James Bond Annual, featuring photos of Sean Connery playing golf. I studied this book whenever I could. I'd collected James Bond bubble-gum cards. ('I'll swap you *Dr No*'s Dragon for your Pussy Galore.') But I'd never seen a Bond film, let alone an Ian Fleming novel. My mother disapproved of Bond, and sex generally. After going to see *Goldfinger* with my Auntie Joan she tried to put me off Bond by claiming that 007 was a nasty man who went to bed with women, did rude things to them and then shot them. Why on earth she thought this would put me off Bond was totally beyond me.

When I arrived at the cinema to see my first James Bond film, I felt, truly felt, that my life was beginning. As the lights went out and that world-famous theme music throbbed through the auditorium, I was so thrilled that my knees shook.

From the moment that Bond punched the man dressed as a woman and throttled him with a poker, to the clumsily speeded-up climactic fight on board Emilio Largo's yacht, this was my story. What was more, it was M's story. Every time Bond said or did something callous, my father, along with all the other dads in the cinema, laughed out loud.

Par example: Bond is talking to Domino on the beach, when a villain called Vargas sneaks up behind them. Bond swivels round and fires a harpoon at Vargas. The harpoon pins Vargas to a tree. Then Bond says: 'I think he got the point.' *(All the dads laugh.)*

In another scene, Bond is on a dancefloor with a villainess called Fiona Volpe. One of Fiona's thugs is prowling behind the stage, hoping to shoot Bond dead. At the last moment, Bond spots the gunman and spins Fiona round, so that she dies of the bullet that was meant for 007. *(All the dads laugh.)*

It was the same when I beat up Lee Farmer. Lee Farmer was a boy I went to school with. One day, when he ratted on a friend of mine, I attacked Farmer outside Biology, and made his nose bleed. His mother came round to our house and complained, threatening to bring the matter to the attention of the headmaster. My mother was concerned. When M came home, he approached me sternly and said: 'So you gave him a fourpenny one, did you?' I nodded sheepishly. To my amazement, M laughed and slapped me on the back. 'Good lad.'

'Myles!' said my mum disapprovingly.

'What?' laughed M. 'He's horrible, that Farmer kid. Ugh!'

My heart swelled with pride. I was not only licensed to kill. I was licensed to beat up Lee Farmer. I imagined M standing behind me while I disembowelled Farmer in the school playground. Then I'd turn to M, point to my enemy's entrails and say: 'He had lots of guts.' *(All the dads in the playground laugh.)*

My brother had always shared M's interest in football and cricket. But my brother was too in love with Bobby Charlton to care about James Bond. The Bond films were something that I, alone, shared with M. And when he took me to see *Thunderball*, he wasn't merely offering me a couple of hours of entertainment. He was initiating me into his world of danger and espionage. He was saying: 'I can't shoot people or make love to three exotic women per film. Your mother wouldn't like it. But you can, son. You're the kind of good-looking bastard who can get all the women he wants. You know all about champagne and fast cars and guns. You're ruthless, with a high tolerance of pain. Go on. Be my guest. I'm making you my top agent. I'm giving you a licence to kill.'

A few days later, I stole a paperback copy of *Thunderball* from my local newsagent, and was delighted to learn that the film had adhered quite closely to the plot of the novel. The book also contained my first ever sex scene, although I didn't recognise it as such at the time. At the end of Chapter 18, Bond unfastens Domino's brassière, and kicks off his bathing trunks. Then, at the beginning of Chapter 19, Bond stares into Domino's face and says: 'I'm sorry. I shouldn't have done that.'

For years, I thought that Bond was apologising for being rude enough to take his trunks off in front of a girl.

My mother, however, obviously knew why Bond had taken his trunks off. While I was at school, she took my prized possession, my stolen copy of *Thunderball* with photographs of Sean Connery and underwater battles on the cover, and incinerated it on the Park-Ray fire in our living room. When my mother boasted about what she'd done, at first I thought she was bluffing. But the next morning, searching through the ashes in the grate, I found a charred but still recognisable remnant of the paperback's cover that said it cost six shillings in Australia. I was outraged.

I told my Auntie Joan what had happened, omitting to mention that the book was stolen. Joan lived next door. She wasn't my real auntie, but she liked me enough to present me with her entire collection of Bond paperbacks: *From Russia With Love*, *Goldfinger*, *Live And Let Die*, *Thunderball*, *Dr No* and *On Her Majesty's Secret Service*. 'Make sure your mum doesn't see them,' she counselled.

All six books fitted safely and neatly under the lid of a board game that was kept in my room, and which no one ever played. It was the greatest hiding place that any child had ever devised: further proof that I was one hell of a field operative.

Night after night, I re-read those novels. I was astonished by how much Fleming seemed to know about me.

Like Bond, I was never quite naked. I was always 'naked except for a towel' or 'naked except for a full school uniform'. Also like Bond, I was a connoisseur of food and drink. I drank only Bulmer's Woodpecker Cider, served at a temperature of 68 degrees F. On assignment, I ate well; Bassett's Licorice Allsorts, then a Mars Bar, ending with a packet of Smoky Bacon especially made for me by Golden Wonder, the crisp people.

As a teenager, well versed in the Bond books, my eyes became 'fierce slits' whenever I was about to kiss a girl. 'What's up with your eyes?' girls would ask me.

'Nothing,' I'd reply, as 'my mouth came down ruthlessly' on theirs.

In keeping with the promotional trailer for *Goldfinger*, I combined my schoolwork with 'girls and thrills, girls and fun, girls and danger'. (Let's not forget the danger.) But whereas Bond had a different woman for every mission, I remained pathetically faithful to my girlfriends and was always heartbroken when they dumped me.

In 1971, something went badly wrong between M and me. After loving the film of *On Her Majesty's Secret Service*, with its dramatic ski chases and wonderful John Barry score, we went to see *Diamonds Are Forever*. The film was full of weak jokes and tedious chases. M and I weren't just disappointed. We were *bored*. Not as bored, perhaps, as Sean Connery, who had been enticed back to the role of Bond for a percentage and a large fee, and now looked more like someone's bad-tempered dad than Fleming's super-hero.

With the arrival of Roger Moore, things went from bad to worse. Now I had to watch myself being played by a man whose bottom got bigger and whose trousers grew browner with each successive film. *Live And Let Die*, Moore's first film as 007, was the last James Bond film I went to see with my father. It was also the last time that we went to the cinema together, ever.

I blame Roger Moore.

In the eighties, M's health began to fail. He had a heart bypass operation and was fitted with plastic arteries.

I blame Roger Moore for that, too.

M was generally a fair man, who hated injustice. I remember a time when my mother found a page from a Bond book I'd been trying to write, and showed it to M on his return from work, calling it 'Percy Filth'. I recall being surprised by how angry he sounded as he turned on her and said: 'Ivy, don't criticise things you don't understand.' I realised then that M didn't simply regard me as a cold and efficient killing machine. He thought I was an *artist*.

When M was unfair, he usually had a good excuse. Like the night that he came home from work and raged at me like a madman for leaving my shoes in the hall. I didn't know it at the time, but he'd just lost his job. My father, who had frequently worked evenings and weekends for no overtime to keep his firm afloat, got the blame for their poor profits and was summarily fired.

After that, M returned to the trade he had learned before the war. He became a humble signwriter. In the discomfort of his own living room, he painted BUY YOUR AUDI AT TAYLOR'S OF HANDFORTH in letters a foot high. But the smell of the paint made my mum ill. So M, not wishing to inconvenience her further, retired altogether.

Two months before James was born, M suffered a stroke, which paralysed the right side of his body and destroyed his ability to speak. The old sailor's face that had never been to sea became distorted and lopsided, and when he tried to talk, nothing emerged but strangled gibberish. He was now a patient at Cherry Tree Hospital, our present destination.

We weren't sure whether Dad understood that he'd become a grandfather or not. The stroke he'd suffered had been severe. I'd sent back photographs of James, which Mum claimed Dad wouldn't allow out of his sight, but this may have been wishful thinking on her part.

But there was no mistaking M's delight when he first saw James. His eyes widened and he began to quake with excited laughter. 'Are you? Are you?' he asked, looking at me and Tracy but pointing at the baby, who was asleep in his carry cot.

'Yes, Dad,' I answered, mock-cheerful. 'We are. We're his parents.' Dad laughed again but it was impossible to say whether he got the joke, or was merely afraid of looking like an uncomprehending stroke victim.

But M knew that the baby was his grandson and certainly didn't require the elaborate mime that Mum provided for him, accompanied by staccato bursts of pidgin English. Waving her arms about like an incompetent cheer leader, she said: 'This baby . . . John and Tracy's baby . . . your grandson . . . called James.' When Mum had completed her performance, Dad turned to Tracy and me to raise his one good eyebrow in disbelief.

Tracy lifted the baby out of his carry cot without waking him and laid him across the old man's lap. For a full hour M sat there, joyfully mesmerised, James's head resting in the crook of his left arm. Dad had always loved children. Every five minutes, Mum held out her arms and said: 'Have you had enough, M? Shall I take him?' Each time she spoke, M shook his head crossly and tightened his grip on his sulking grandson.

Finally a nurse arrived to inform us that it was time for M's physiotherapy. Would we mind leaving? At this, M started to cry, not like a sick old man, but like a small child having a tantrum. I had to prise his sticky fingers off the baby while Tracy promised M that we would be back soon. Mum tried to defuse the situation with another display of semaphore. Dad responded by blowing a loud raspberry. Although the stroke meant that he had lost the power of speech, his ability to blow raspberries was mercifully unimpaired.

'Myles, what are you doing? It's me. Ivy! I'm here to help you. We all are.' Mum wept as we steered her towards the exit.

'Are you?' M shouted after us, his lined face flooded with angry tears. 'Are you, are you? *Are you?*'

3

Muckraker

When we got home, I tried to lose myself in work. Not an easy task, as my work utilised a pitifully small number of brain cells. I still wrote copy for Bill's Agency, working from home and sending my crap down the net. It was me who coined that infamous slogan for Brogan's Irish Bitter: 'When you taste it, it won't seem expensive at all, at all, at all'. (I also suggested a better slogan that they didn't use: 'Brogan's needs no slogans'.)

My most celebrated coup was thinking of a winning line for Sony in the mid-eighties, when every electronics company in the world was competing for a share of the personal stereo market. The mantra I came up with, 'Only the Sony' appeared in magazines and on billboards all over the English-speaking world.

Tracy thinks I should have taken legal action against Bill for claiming he'd thought of the Sony slogan himself. I might have done, had I been able to afford a decent lawyer. But I'd always known what Bill was like, ever since a student party in '81.

That night I passed out after a heavy drinking session, then awoke to find Bill shagging my girlfriend, who was mercifully unconscious at the time. So you see, sueing Bill would have been like putting my hand in a lion's mouth, then sueing the lion for biting it off.

Besides, I'd been feeling a bit sorry for Bill lately. Business had taken quite a nosedive since the boom of the eighties. At work, his motto had always been: 'Money first, integrity later'. Bill seriously believed that there would be plenty of time for philanthropy when he retired; indeed, that he could only afford to be generous in the future if he shafted everybody in the present.

Lately, however, Bill had become the shaftee rather than the shafter. His recent divorce had robbed him of his Surrey mansion and his new Ferrari. Now he was forced to slum it in a Saab. Most of the accounts that came his way nowadays were insultingly small-time.

For example: I was currently working with an American mail-order clothing company who wanted their catalogue to be adapted for the English market. This involved changing descriptions like 'this neat squall jacket in cherry, tan and black' to 'this stylish windcheater in red, brown and black'.

Mostly, I wasn't mad at Bill because I didn't want to work in advertising any more. I wanted to do something useful with my life. I'd reached my late-thirties without achieving anything more than a few catchy slogans which, let's face it, isn't much to brag about. Besides, I had more important things to worry about than Bill.

My chances of being nominated for the Father of the Year

Award were still looking decidedly slim. I didn't resent the fact that James had been born – not even in my bitterest moments. What I regretted was my continuing inability to take pleasure in his company. Being in the same room as James made me feel as if I was about to explode. The inner pressure was incredible.

I was seething with anger, but I knew I had no cause to be angry with my child. Nor could I blame his mother for wanting a baby so badly, and loving him so devotedly since his arrival. So my entire body was charged with a slow, malignant rage that had no target and no outlet.

By the time the baby was two months old, Tracy and I had developed a daily routine. In the morning, I would sleep until eleven while Tracy looked after James. Then I'd get up, have breakfast, shower and dress, and spend the afternoon and early evening working or reading Bond novels in my study – while Tracy looked after James. (After an extensive tour of all the charity shops in West London, I had reassembled my collection of Bond paperbacks, including all the editions with film tie-in covers.)

At about seven, I'd have dinner with Tracy. Then return to my study until she and the baby were asleep, when I'd venture into the living room to drink a few beers and watch a Bond film before bed. I now owned the entire series on video, and knew beyond a shadow of a doubt that *Goldfinger* was the best Bond film ever. *The Man With The Golden Gun* (I blame Roger Moore) was the worst.

OHMSS had the best music and the most spectacular action sequences. The most exciting fight appeared in *From Russia With Love*, between Red Grant and Bond on the Orient Express. The most gorgeous women were Ursula Andress in *Dr No*, Carole Bouquet in *For Your Eyes Only* and Maryam D'Abo in *The Living Daylights*. The fattest bottom belonged to Roger Moore in *Octopussy*.

George Lazenby may have been raw and inexperienced. But out of all the actors who've played Bond, Lazenby was the only man to rival Connery in the testosterone department. Early one morning, I was watching George cradle his dead wife in his arms when Tracy, holding James, walked into my line of vision, switched off the TV and turned to face me.

I said: 'What did you do that for?'

She gazed at me frankly. 'I'm depressed, if you really want to know.'

Mollified, I said: 'I don't blame you. That has to be the saddest moment in any of the Bond films.'

Tracy tutted in disgust. 'Oh, grow up, you prick.' She sat down and started to feed the baby with a bottle of formula milk that we'd brought back from Stockport. She'd been forced to abandon breast feeding a few days ago because her milk had dried up. 'I'm not depressed about your stupid bloody video! I'm depressed about us.'

I had no idea what she was talking about, and said so.

Tracy started crying. 'I love you. Why are you being like this?'

'What do you mean?' I said, knowing full well what she meant.

'I mean "What's wrong with you?" Why won't you look at your own son?' She shook James sharply. He wowled indignantly, then resumed feeding.

'Hey. Don't be so rough with him.'

'Why? What do you care?'

'Of course I care. And I *do* look at him. I'm looking at him now.'

'Only because he's right in front of your big fucking nose.'

'Tracy, he's a lovely boy. I'm very fond of him.'

'Are you?'

'You sound like my dad,' I said carelessly.

With this, Tracy's spirit seemed to ignite. 'I'll bet you're having an affair!'

'What's my dad got to do with having an affair?'

'You are, aren't you? You're shagging someone!'

'Tracy. How could I be shagging someone? I never go anywhere. Who could I be shagging? The old woman at the OXFAM shop?'

She seemed to see the logic of this. 'Well, what's wrong, then? Have you stopped loving me? What is it? Just tell me. Because you've been a real bastard since James came home.'

I knew she was right, but argued anyway, as if arguing had been written into my contract. 'Why? What've I done?'

'Nothing!' she spat. 'That's just the point.'

'But I thought we'd agreed. You look after James while I carry on working.'

'Who gives a shit what we agreed?' she blazed. 'I thought it'd be different when you saw him. I thought you'd love him so much that nothing else would matter. It didn't happen, did it?'

'No,' I said quietly.

'I thought you'd be a wonderful dad. But it's been like living with a different person since he was born. I've cried myself to sleep every night, I've been so unhappy.'

'Tracy, I didn't know that.'

'No. Because you were always in here, watching fucking James Bond videos. You've made me so miserable, John. I've been more exhausted than I've ever been in my life, and all you've done is shut yourself off and ignore me. You're doing it now. Look at you.' She shuddered. 'How can you be so cold?'

I shrugged with an indifference that I did not feel. I was inwardly thrilled. Tracy had unwittingly quoted a sentence from *Goldeneye*. Calmly, not fluffing my lines at all, I replied: 'It's what keeps me alive.'

During the scene in which this exchange occurs, Natalya, Bond's girl-for-the-movie, is criticising Bond's resolve to hunt down the villain. Like most women, Natalya doesn't believe that some people are innately evil, and that there is really nothing to be done with such vermin but to eliminate them. After I'd said: 'It's what keeps me alive,' it would have been particularly effective if Tracy, in turn, had intoned Natalya's answer: 'It's what keeps you alone.'

This was out of the question, however. Tracy hadn't seen *Goldeneye*, or watched any Bond film all the way through.

She screamed in frustration. 'See? That's exactly the kind of thing I mean.' She put the bottle down and began to pat James's back. 'You're not even making sense any more. "It's what keeps me alive." What in Christ's name is that supposed to mean?'

'Tracy,' I said firmly, in a voice and manner that I scarcely recognised as my own. 'If I'm talking crap, it's because I don't know what else to say.' I took a deep breath. 'OK. I admit that I've found it very hard since the baby came home. It's been a bit of a shock. OK? That honest enough for you?'

James burped loudly. Tracy blew her nose and dried her eyes.

'Three of us,' I continued. 'In this tiny flat . . . I'm finding it claustrophobic. But he's still my son. I would have thought it was obvious that I care about him.'

'Why? Why's it obvious? You've never fed him or bathed him. You haven't changed a single nappy since he was born. You don't wash his clothes, you don't rock him to sleep. You don't get up in the night when he cries. You hardly ever pick him up. You don't even look at him unless you have to. What's fucking obvious about it?'

'I sing to him,' I said feebly.

'Yes,' she sneered. 'I've heard you. You sing *Goldfinger* to him.'

'No,' I retorted indignantly. 'Not just *Goldfinger*. I sing all the best Bond themes to him.'

'Oh, wow. The perfect father.' She shook her head sadly and sighed. 'John, why don't you just admit it? You've been useless. Absolutely bloody useless.'

'Tracy, maybe I am useless. But I didn't want to be a father in the first place.'

'I know,' she conceded, her shoulders slumped in defeat.

I said: 'It was you who wanted a baby. I thought being a parent would be depressing and I was right. It's exactly as bloody awful as I thought it'd be. I only agreed to the whole stupid idea because I couldn't bear seeing you so unhappy.'

She smiled sadly. 'And how happy do you think I am now?' There was a question on my mind that I was afraid to ask. But I asked it anyway. 'Are you going to leave me?'

She shook her head and laughed through her tears. 'Am I hell!'

I felt relieved but guilty. In spite of my myriad faults, Tracy loved me so much that she could scarcely contemplate life without me.

She laughed again. 'Dickbrain,' she said affectionately.

'That's my name,' I admitted.

'Is it so hard to understand? *I just want you to be nice to me.*'

Thinking that the crisis was over, I reached out to touch her. She pushed my arm away. I ought to have anticipated this. Tracy's finest trait was her reluctance to condemn people. Her worst trait was her reluctance to forgive them once she'd condemned them. 'Tracy,' I whined. 'I can't be nice to you if you won't be nice back.'

The baby stopped belching and started to cry.

I walked over to the video recorder, ejected *OHMSSS* and replaced the cassette in its Special Limited Edition Collector's Item Gift Box. I turned to see Tracy lifting James off her lap. She looked terrified.

'John,' she gasped.

I rushed over to her. James was still crying. He was threshing his arms and legs, frantically trying to swallow air. As we watched, his face changed colour, from red to blue and then to purple. He was suffocating.

'Christ! What can we do?' breathed Tracy.

Without answering, I rushed out to the hall and rang for an ambulance.

When I returned to the living room, James was lying on the sofa. His mother was kneeling over him. He was limp and motionless, his head turned helplessly towards us. He was paler than any living thing I'd ever seen, but he was still breathing. Tracy, surprisingly calm and contained, was stroking the baby's head and making soothing noises. There was a solemn look on his small white face, as if he'd glimpsed truths that no infant should be party to.

A dark notion drifted into my head, the idea that this was somehow my doing, that my poisonous resentment had almost snuffed out a child's life. ('Mister Bryce? This is your wake-up call.')

The truth was, the boy needed a father. Tracy needed a husband.

There was only one man for the job.

4

On Her Majesty's National Health Service

James was rushed to the Children's Accident and Emergency Department at the Chelsea and Westminster Hospital, where a weary junior doctor listened to his chest and detected a heart murmur. This diagnosis didn't trouble Tracy and me unduly. 'Heart murmur' sounds like a feeble complaint that mumbles threats under its breath, lacking the courage to come right out and admit it's trying to kill you. A cousin of mine had a heart murmur, and all it seemed to mean was that his heart beat was sometimes slightly erratic. Surely nobody died from having a lousy sense of rhythm? Besides, the colour had returned to James's cheeks. Perhaps all he'd suffered was a bad bout of indigestion?

An ambulance ferried us across London to Bloomsbury, home of Great Ormond Street Hospital, where they had better scanning equipment. I first heard of this hospital when I myself was a child and opened the novel of *Peter Pan*. ('Did you know that J. M. Barrie's royalty on this book goes to help sick children at the Great Ormond Street Hospital for Sick Children?') As a ten-year-old, I remember feeling a virtuous glow in my belly as I read these lines, while being surprised that there were so many sick children that they needed a special hospital to put them in.

Barrie's presence still looms large at Great Ormond Street, in the chapel where a plaque commemorates his generosity and in the Peter Pan café, where the food is so bad that any child who eats there is guaranteed never to grow up.

In spite of the pain and the heartbreak that the staff, parents and patients experience on a daily basis, the hospital is a curiously welcoming place, with a warmth that embraces you as soon as you walk through its automatic doors into its bright, buzzing entrance hall.

First of all, James was weighed and measured. Then he was taken to the echocardiography department, to have his heart scanned. With Tracy carrying the baby, we entered a small office where the ultra-sound scan was performed by an imperious young brunette. She was wearing a tight white blouse through which her taut breasts made their impudent presence felt. She gave us a perfunctory smile and introduced herself as Dr Phelps. What was her accent? American? No, Canadian. I recognised the nasal twang of Quebec.

James, naked except for his nappy, lay on a long narrow couch while Dr Phelps smeared some kind of conductive jelly over his chest. Tracy and I sat side by side, holding hands, on the opposite side of the couch to the doctor. After dimming the lights, she began to move a probe over his chest. A number of alarming, indistinct monochrome images appeared on a TV monitor, accompanied by a rhythmic wush-wush-wush that was obviously the sound of my son's heart.

'Can you see anything?' asked Tracy innocently.

Dr Phelps grunted non-commitally, without shifting her gaze from the screen. She offered no explanation for the images we were seeing, merely took print-outs as she went along. Another young woman entered the office and peered into the screen.

Dr Phelps greeted her colleague, then pointed to what looked like a psychedelic vortex from a cheap sixties film. 'What do you think?' she said, as if Tracy and I weren't in the room. 'PASD, small left ventricle and aorta, leaky mitral valve but I can't find a narrowing of the aorta.'

The other woman had a bash, but couldn't find a narrowing of the aorta either.

I was rapidly losing patience. 'Would you mind telling us what's going on?'

My question seemed to startle Dr Phelps. 'Oh. Well, we've found a PASD . . .'

Tracy said: 'A what?'

'A Partial Atrial Septal Defect.'

My face was dark and watchful as I said: 'We still don't know what you're talking about.'

Dr Phelps's colleague gave me an unctuous 'Yes, terribly confusing, isn't it?' smile. 'A hole in the heart,' she announced brightly, as if we'd won some kind of prize. 'She's got a hole in the heart. Between the two upper chambers, to be precise.'

I said: 'She's a boy, to be precise.'

Dr Phelps held up one of the print-outs and pointed to a fuzzy patch of grey. 'Right here. See?'

'That doesn't prove a thing,' I retorted.

Dr Phelps laughed. She thought I was joking. 'Well. Take it from me . . . the hole's there. Also, the left side of the heart is significantly smaller than the right. Given these defects . . .'

'I beg your pardon?' I said.

'Er, defects?'

'Sorry,' I said. My eyes became fierce slits. 'You were talking about my son, but for a second there, I could have sworn you said "defects".'

Tracy nudged me with her elbow. Not knowing how to respond, Dr Phelps persevered: 'Well, normally, when we see these, er, problems with a child, we expect to see a narrowing of the aorta. But I've checked and double-checked, and can find no such narrowing. The aorta *is* a little small, but it doesn't taper . . .'

I said: 'That's good, then, isn't it?'

Dr Phelps sighed and wiped the jelly off the baby's chest with a green paper towel. I suddenly pictured her at home, eating a takeaway in front of the TV. But she didn't look any friendlier, not even in my imagination. She excused herself and walked out, taking the images of James's heart with her. Her accomplice retreated to the other side of the room and began to thumb through a thick wad of mail.

Tracy cuddled the baby and wept silently. I had no idea what to say, so I simply put my arms around her. After a few minutes, Dr Phelps returned with her consultant, a cheerful man with white hair and a sensitive, angular face.

'I'm Dr Mervyn,' he said. 'Nice to see you. I do mean that.'

'No one said you didn't,' I reminded him sourly. The good doctor ignored me.

Playfully, he pressed his face close to James's. 'Well, you're a bit of a puzzle, aren't you, hmmm?' Then he took out his stethoscope and examined the baby with minute precision, listening to his heart and checking the pulses on his arms and inner thighs. Gradually, Dr Mervyn's good cheer evaporated. His pale Celtic face grew pensive and sad. He put away his stethoscope and sighed. After a long pause, he spoke.

'Well folks, I don't think we can leave this little one hanging around for much longer.' He shook his head. 'I think we'd better keep him in. Don't you? I think it'd be for the best . . .'

'Is he very ill?' said Tracy.

'Yes. I'm afraid so. He's got quite a sizeable hole between the two upper receiving chambers of his heart,' began Dr Mervyn, directing his attention exclusively at my wife. 'This hole allows unoxygenated blood to pass backwards and forwards between the two chambers before it reaches the lungs. So basically, the heart has to work a lot harder than it should. Looking at him, I'd say he's going to need an operation pretty soon.'

Tracy sobbed loudly. Dr Phelps passed her a paper tissue. I maintained a watchful, taciturn silence.

'I am sorry. Really I am,' said Dr Mervyn, as if he meant it. 'Normally, we don't like to operate until they're four or five. The older, the better. But this little chap can't wait that long. I realise this must all have come as a bit of a shock for you. I'm terribly sorry.'

* * *

We were despatched to Room 4 of the Richard Bonham Carter ward, on the fifth floor of the hospital's cardiac wing. We slept beside James's cot on a lumpy old camp bed. Meanwhile, the nursing staff attempted to stabilise his condition by giving him tube feeds and drugs. The cardiologists needed to see a marked improvement in his weight and general health before they could risk subjecting him to major surgery.

Personally, I could see nothing wrong with James. With his huge dark eyes and rather ruthless smile, he looked as if he was positively thriving. But Tracy had little faith in my opinion. When I voiced my concerns to her on our first night in the hospital, she argued with me so bitterly that I pretended to agree with her, just to keep the peace.

In uncompaniable silence, we returned to the ward, only to face a new horror. Tracy's parents had turned up for an impromptu visit. We entered Room 4 to find them both leaning over James's cot. The baby was smiling in his sleep, quite oblivious to the heartache he was causing.

Florence, convinced that her grandchild was doomed, was weeping discreetly into a small flowered handkerchief. Patrick dithered unhelpfully at her side, holding a vast thermos picnic bag, his face cremation grey.

'What are you doing here?' demanded Tracy, unable to hide her displeasure.

Ingratiatingly, Florence snatched the picnic bag from her husband and half-opened it, inviting us to peer inside. 'We've brought a hot meal. Eating in these hospital canteens can be a wee bit dicey . . .'

Patrick nodded in absent-minded agreement.

'It's a roast dinner,' beamed Florence. She paused to blow her nose. She smiled at me and pinched Tracy's cheek affectionately. 'You always loved roast dinners, even when you were a little girl . . .'

'Oh,' said Tracy, disarmed and deflated. 'Thanks, Mum.'

'That's really kind,' I conceded grudgingly.

Reassured, Florence sank into a chair. She bent over and reached into the bag, producing a foil-covered dinner plate which she laid on her lap. Then she removed the foil to expose a plate containing roasted potatoes, peas, brussel sprouts, sausages, Yorkshire pudding and lean roast beef. Next, she unscrewed a small thermos flask and tipped steaming gravy over the food. Wrinkling up her nose coquettishly, she presented the plate to Tracy, along with a knife and fork.

'God, this looks great,' enthused Tracy, settling down to eat.

Patrick and Florence stood over their daughter, smiling indulgently, convinced that for once, they had done the right thing. The smell of the food was making me hungry. I decided to serve myself and reached for the picnic bag. But it was empty. Tracy saw my confusion and already fearing the worst, stared up at her mother. 'Mum, you haven't.'

Florence looked blank. 'What? What?'

Blushing with emotion, Tracy said: 'Where's John's dinner?'

Patrick's mouth drooped at the corners. He stepped back sharply as if fearing physical violence. Florence affected polite surprise. 'Oh,' she said innocently. 'Would John have liked a meal as well?'

I sighed. 'Oh, for God's sake . . .'

Tracy put down her plate. 'Mum, this has been the worst week of our lives. Of *course* John would have liked a meal!'

Shaking with emotion, Tracy got to her feet and walked out of the room.

'Oh dear,' said Florence. 'Is she upset?'

I shook my head despairingly and went after Tracy. I found her on the stairs, sobbing her heart out. I sat down beside her and took her hand. 'Take it easy, Tracy.'

'They're monsters, John,' she sobbed. 'Make them go away . . .'

A sister from the ward, a West Indian woman with a face that was at once gentle and fierce, descended the stairs and knelt beside us. 'Anything I can do?'

Dispensing with the minor details, I told her about Tracy's parents. The sister listened calmly without interrupting. Then she said: 'Well, look. If they're making you feel *this* bad, it'd be quite a simple matter for me to tell them their visits aren't helping you or your baby. Do you want me to do that?'

Tracy seemed uncertain, so I took the initiative. 'Would you? We'd be extremely grateful.'

'No problem,' affirmed the sister solemnly.

When we returned to Room 4, Tracy's parents had gone. The plate of food rested on the floor, where Tracy had left it. Tracy had lost her appetite, so I finished the meal myself. It was greasy and cold, but I was too hungry to care.

The next morning, Tracy and I made a special effort to be nice to each other. Tracy encouraged me to rock my son to sleep, a task I actually came to enjoy. While James rested, we walked around the hospital, hand in hand, strangely at peace with each other and the hostile fate that had brought us here.

But living in a hospital room for twenty-four hours a day is a demoralising affair. The doctors visit twice a day, once in the morning and again in the evening. The nurses turn up hourly, to take the baby's temperature and check its heart rate. In between these visits, absolute silence reigns. A hospital silence is unique in that it cannot be filled by music or conversation or even a blaring television. Sometimes, you'll do anything to get away from that deathly hush.

My escape method involved frequent and often quite unnecessary trips to the hospital shop or the supermarket: anything to ease the strain and boredom of living on a ward. Tracy was unwilling to leave James's side, so running countless errands for her became an ingenious way of indulging myself while appearing to indulge my wife. On our fifth evening, Tracy voiced a craving for some plain Lindt chocolate. 'You wait here,' I instructed. 'I'll go and get you some.'

In the daytime, the foyer of Great Ormond Street teems with people. Children in wheelchairs, arriving and departing, wait by the front reception desk with their parents and their nurses. Whole families (mothers behaving normally, fathers moody and silent) come and go constantly.

The only permanent fixture is a lonely old woman who sits outside the café. She keeps office hours, from nine until five each day, sucking sweets and chatting to anyone who happens to be sitting near by. She isn't there to visit anyone. She's merely passing the time. The hospital is her substitute for a social life.

At night, when the hospital shop and café are closed and the old woman has gone home, the foyer grows empty and still. Apart from the parents making dutiful phonecalls to their friends and relatives ('She's doing very well. She starts chemotherapy tomorrow.'), all is silent. That was why, as I walked past two people standing by the entrance, I was able to hear one of them say: 'It's been a great pleasure, Mr Shatterheart.'

I glanced back at the speaker, a tall, middle-aged woman wearing an expensive overcoat. She was shaking hands with a man of middle height who somehow contrived to appear taller than her by virtue of his erect military bearing. Feeling my eyes upon him, the man glanced at me incuriously, then turned back to his companion.

I caught a fleeting impression of a slit-like mouth, authority and cruelty in its thin, downturned lips. The eyes behind the thick spectacle lenses blazed with inimical power. It was the cleverest, most unambiguously evil face that I had ever seen.

My pulse raced as I walked to the convenience store in the neighbouring street. Good God above! So that was Shatterheart! As the consultant cardiothoracic surgeon, Shatterheart was the man most likely to operate on James. But how could that be? One only had to look at the surgeon to see that he was drunk with power and bloodlust. He was positively certifiable!

At the store I bought some chocolate, a bottle of vodka, some vermouth and tonic. At the checkout I paused to survey the cigarettes stacked above the counter. 'Do you sell Morland

Specials?' I said. The man behind the till shook his head impassively. 'What you see is what we got.'

I saw his gaze fall to my chest and realised that he was looking at my 'resident parent' security tag, the badge that I wore permanently to show that I was not on the hospital premises to steal drugs or babies.

'OK,' I said. 'Give me twenty Consulate.'

I was perfectly aware that James Bond didn't smoke mentholated cigarettes. Consulate was the brand that I had smoked, or tried to smoke, when I was thirteen. Since then, every five years or so, I had been moved to buy a pack, hoping that the mint-flavoured smoke would act like a Proustian biscuit, evoking my childhood and more importantly, all the happiness and confidence that the intervening years had crushed. So far, my occasional habit had evoked nothing but a sore throat and a powerful sense of self-disgust.

Charmlessly, the cashier slapped a pack of Consulate down on the counter. 'And have you any black oxidised Ronson lighters in stock, by any chance?'

He shook his head robustly, as if he suspected me of mocking him. He pointed at the matches. 'What you see . . .'

'Is what you got,' I rejoined ironically. 'Fine. I'll take a box of Swan Vestas.'

On my way back to the hospital, I wondered why I'd bought cigarettes. After all, I didn't smoke. When I entered the hospital, Shatterheart and the woman had gone. The phone at reception rang urgently and almost immediately, the attractive female security officer behind the desk called out to me.

'Mr Bond!'

I turned and stared at her. 'I beg your pardon?'

She gave me a warm smile of appraisal and held the receiver aloft for me. It was a red telephone. Of course! The red telephone that had always been 007's direct link with headquarters.

I slowly walked towards her, feeling the familiar charge of excitement that had heralded so many exciting assignments. After accepting the receiver, I pressed it to my ear. 'Hello?' I said.

There was a lengthy silence.

Then I heard a muffled voice say: 'Are you? Are you? Are you?'

5

Number 007

There was no time to say goodbye to Tracy.

I caught the last train to Stockport and travelled to Cherry Tree Hospital by taxi. It was 1.25 a.m., as I walked through the grim hospital ward for this top-secret briefing from my father. There were no other visitors. M and I were alone together for the first time since his stroke.

Approaching my father's bed, I immediately noticed a change in him. Whereas previously, M had spent his days perched on top of his bed, propped up with pillows like a carefully balanced ventriloquist's dummy, he was now sitting in a swivel chair with his back to me.

As I placed the obligatory grapes on the bed, the paper bag that contained them rustled. M spun round in his chair and glared at me. I swore under my breath. The complexion that had recently been as grey as the ashes of *Thunderball* was now ruddy and weatherbeaten again. The eyes that had looked so bloodshot and unfocused had returned to their former state of damnable clarity. The pipe that was forever going out was once again cupped in his left palm. And when I offered M my hand – during his illness, this most reserved of men had held my hand on a regular basis – he drew back in surprise and disgust. This was more like it!

I sat down on the bed and gave the old man what I hoped was a smile of friendship. 'Are you, are you?' I asked encouragingly.

'Don't be so damned patronising.' I went cold with shock. 'I'm not ready to be put out to grass, yet . . .'

'Dad?' Had I been capable of tears, I would have wept. 'You can talk. I don't believe it. You got better!'

He shook his head kindly but firmly. 'Stuff and nonsense. I'm never going to get better. You know that as well as I do. The stroke I had was a pretty major one. Caused irreparable damage to the left cerebral hemisphere of my brain.' He puffed ruminatively on his pipe for a few moments. 'Now, the left hemisphere – the left cerebellum to be exact – governs our rational side, and is responsible for turning thoughts into language. In my case, the left cerebellum's been dealt the equivalent of a blow from a twenty-pound hammer. In other words, I can still think rationally, but my left brain merely takes all my perfectly sensible thoughts and turns them into verbal twaddle. Hence all this "are you? are you?" nonsense. Do you follow?'

I nodded. M's eyes glittered as he warmed to his theme. 'Which brings me to this little marvel . . .' He tapped the bowl of his pipe against my knee. 'May look like a common-or-garden briar pipe, may even smoke like one. But, in fact, it's a digital DLCDD.'

'A what?'

'A damaged left cerebellum decoding device. Amazing what these chaps at Q Branch think up. Major Boothroyd brought it over after supper. Couldn't wait to show off his latest toy. Means I can now talk to you and be clearly understood. Blessed relief.' A warning glint entered the cold, shrewd eyes. 'However, I needn't remind you that for security reasons, this interview is classified. As far as the rest of humanity – your mother included – is concerned, I'm conversationally defunct and shall remain so. To ensure that I don't weaken, the decoder will self-destruct in ten minutes from now. Understood?'

I said: 'I must be dreaming.' This, of course, is exactly what James Bond said when Honor Blackman said: 'My name is Pussy Galore.' My name, on the other hand, was John Bryce. That fact was unalterable. So what was going on?

M seemed to read my mind. Mildly, he said: 'Don't worry. You're not going mad. Just as you suspected when I took you to see *Thunderball*, I'm in charge of MI6 and you're the real James Bond. Sorry if it's come as a bit of a shock. I was pretty bowled over myself when I found out.'

'Dad. What are you talking about? It's me. John.'

M punched the bed in a sudden fit of temper. 'Who the hell do you think's running this show? Pig-headed young fool! You're 007 and that's an order.'

I was afraid to argue with him. M had gone dangerously red in the face. Knowing that a second stroke would finish the old man off, I decided to play along with him. I focused all of my attention on the calm, lined sailor's face that I knew and loved. 'Now pay attention,' he barked. 'We don't have much time. What do you know about this surgeon chap, Shatterheart?'

'He's the best paediatric surgeon in Europe. Might even be the best in the world. He's going to operate on James. Try to patch up the hole in his heart.'

'Correction.' The hard eyes glinted. 'James hasn't got a hole in his heart.'

'What do you mean?'

'Precisely what I say. Your original instincts were correct, 007. There's nothing wrong with my grandson. A team of the country's finest cardiologists, with this Shatterheart chap at their helm, have been lying through their teeth . . .'

I whistled softly. 'So *that's* the score! I knew no child of mine could be born with a physical imperfection . . .'

M dismissed this preposterous notion with a wave of his pipe. 'And it doesn't stop there. I don't have to tell you what kind of state the Health Service is in . . . no beds, no staff, healthy people going into hospital, dead people coming out.' He waved his pipe at the ward around him. 'Look at this place, for heaven's sake. Health care in Britain is falling apart. Know why?'

'Underfunding, sir?'

M nodded without looking up. His pipe had gone out and he was busily trying to relight it. 'Partly. But that's not the whole reason. Haven't you noticed that the doctors and nurses we do have, from the humblest GP right up to chaps of Shatterheart's calibre, are almost entirely useless?'

'As a matter of fact, I have.'

'Of course, there are still decent doctors and nurses out

there. Just the other day, I was reading about a Dr Solman of Richmond-upon-Thames who hasn't killed a single patient. But on the whole, it's a pretty sorry picture. The Health Service is going to rack and ruin. It's your job to find out why. One thing's for certain . . . whatever's going on, Shatterheart's at the bottom of it.'

Soberly, I said: 'He certainly looks like a Bond villain. But do we have any proof that he and his team are guilty of anything more serious than criminal negligence?'

M's grey eyes glittered. 'Only this: remember that breathless attack that the baby suffered? The result of a poisoned bottle of milk that someone slipped into the baby's changing bag.'

'I knew it!' I exclaimed.

M swivelled in his chair to stare at the window. 'We had the contents of the milk analysed. It contained a tiny amount of sap from the Australian Woolly Woolly bean – enough to kill ten men. But my grandson miraculously survived it.

'Take it from me, 007 – James was meant to die from that seizure. It was attempted murder. Instead, he cheated the grim reaper. The lad's as tough and resilient as his father. Next time, he may not be so lucky . . .'

'Except there won't be a next time . . .' I clenched my fists and gritted my teeth, just like Timothy Dalton when he was over-acting in *Licence To Kill*. M swivelled back to face me. His steely eyes narrowed. 'This is a mission, Commander. If you can't treat it as such, coolly and objectively, I'll get 006 to replace you . . .'

'That might prove a little tricky, sir. I'm afraid 006 turned out to be a double agent. He got squashed at the end of *Goldeneye*.'

M banged his fist down on the bed testily. 'Don't be so damned pedantic, man!'

'Sorry.'

'All I'm saying is that I don't want you getting all emotional on me like you did in *You Only Live Twice*.'

'You're referring to the novel, of course . . .'

'There you go again, dammit!'

'Sorry Dad. I mean, sir.'

'Your job is to observe Mr Shatterheart. Find out what he's up to, then stop him.' The look of cold command in M's eyes left me in no doubt about what I was being ordered to do. The old man had always disliked sending men out to commit murder. He paused and studied me reflectively. 'Any questions?'

'Just one, sir. Wouldn't it be simpler just to refuse to let Shatterheart near the baby? After all, no one can operate on James without parental consent.'

'No. That'd be bound to cause more problems with your ladyfriend.' As he made this vague allusion to my wife, M's mouth turned down at the edges. He had never approved of my womanising. 'She already thinks you're having mental problems. Tell her what I've just told you and she'll have you certified. No. She's convinced that Shatterheart is the answer to her prayers. Let her carry on thinking it. For the time being, at any rate.

'In any case, this isn't just about James. It's about all the people suffering in British hospitals, who don't die of cancer or heart disease, but of incompetence and sheer neglect. No, 007. The country's in one hell of a mess. Words have failed us. It's time for action. Your licence to kill is renewed, as of now.'

M took a slim folder off the bed and passed it to me. It was untitled and lacked the usual top-secret red star. It had been stamped, in red ink, with the words: FOR YOUR EYES ONLY. 'This'll tell you all you need to know,' said M gruffly. 'Read and destroy.'

I got to my feet. 'Yes sir.' M puffed at his pipe, head down, deep in thought. After a few moments he glanced up, irritated to find me still present. 'That'll be all.'

I smiled. 'Not quite all, sir.' Gazing down at the top of my father's head, I said: 'As father and son . . . would you say that you and me, er, that we got on reasonably well?'

M glared at me accusingly. 'What kind of damn' fool question is that?'

'Sorry, sir.' I swallowed loudly. 'I suppose all I'm trying to say is that I love you . . .'

M sat up in his chair and surveyed me with a horror so acute that it was almost comical. Giving him no time to answer, I blustered on. 'I was just wondering . . . what do you think of me? That is, assuming that you've got an opinion? And if you haven't, that's quite all right. But if you do love me, or have any kind of opinion about me at all, well, I wouldn't mind hearing it, Dad . . . just this once . . .'

M's shrewd grey eyes filled with tears. At that instant, the pipe in his hand bleeped loudly and emitted a slow, thin plume of black smoke. He opened his fingers and the pipe clattered to the dull linoleum floor. M's lips were trembling. He suddenly looked lost, old and bewildered.

'Yes, Dad?' I coaxed.

The words, when they came, sounded alien and guttural, as if wrenched from the deepest part of him. *'Are you?'* he said. *'Are you? Are you? Are you?'*

6

The Living Daydreams

In a Bond film, there would have been a taxi or an official car waiting for me outside the hospital. 'Where to, Mr Bond?' 'Oh, just take me for a ride . . .' But the Bond films were cinematic fantasies. So there was no car or taxi, no silver Aston Martin waiting in the hospital car park.

For a child or a teenager, the worst part of any Bond film is walking out of the cinema into the real world. Particularly if you've then got to catch the bus home. It is virtually impossible to pretend that a double-decker bus is an Aston Martin, or that a bus driver is a private chauffeur sent to escort you to Government House.

Having said that, James Bond catches a tram in *The Living Daylights* and drives a double-decker bus in *Live And Let Die*. But in both cases, he has no choice. In *The Living Daylights*, he is trailing the talented cellist Kara Milovy, played by the stunning Maryam d'Abo. In *Live And Let Die*, Bond and Solitaire are being pursued by Mr Big's hoodlums.

All 007 has to do is drive under a low bridge so that the

bus can cleave in two, his pursuers can crash into the wreckage and all the dads can laugh. That's the sole purpose of the sequence. Unlike a real bus driver, he isn't expected to wait at innumerable bus stops to collect drunks or dithering pensioners who have to be helped into their seats. So in *Live And Let Die*, it doesn't seem out of character for 007 to be a bus-driver.

But driving a bus is one thing. Boarding a bus as a passenger and saying: 'The Rising Sun, please' is quite another. In this situation, the only thing an agent can do to preserve a modicum of Bondian dignity is to sit at the back and hum the Bond theme as quietly as possible. Unless any attractive women choose to occupy neighbouring seats. If this happens, silence is by far the best policy. The only thing that women find less attractive than secret agents who ride on buses are secret agents who hum on buses.

In view of these problems, I deemed it advisable to walk home. Also, the last bus had departed hours ago. Bond walks in every one of the films and books, so there was no real shame in this. If I'd been in the mood, I might actually have run. Sean Connery ran in *From Russia With Love* when he was fleeing from an enemy helicopter. He ran less convincingly in *Thunderball* when Fiona and her thugs chased him through the Junkanoo parade. All I can say in his defence is that he'd just been shot in the leg.

George Lazenby ran athletically in *OHMSS*, notably when he was saving Tracy from drowning and when the telephone kiosk he was calling London from was shattered by enemy bullets. Tim Dalton sprinted memorably in the pre-credits sequence for *The Living Daylights*. Pierce Brosnan ran several times in the course of *Goldeneye*. In *For Your Eyes Only*, even Roger Moore ended up running. Although he looked rather poorly while he was doing it.

In short, James Bond only runs when he has to. Unless he is being chased by agents from SMERSH or SPECTRE, it's probably fair to say that he won't run. It's equally unlikely that he'll catch the bus. Had he been in my shoes, rather than the camp black moccasins that Ian Fleming makes him wear, I'm fairly certain that Bond would have walked. Whether he would have walked through Hazel Grove at two in the morning is another matter.

Hazel Grove village was deserted. The pubs had emptied and boarded up their doors. The most suicidal of their clients would now be in Hazel Grove's only nightclub, the hideous Bamboo club, where a broken bottle in the face was offered to all customers, free of charge. I had never been there. I had merely seen the ambulances parked outside.

I passed Commercial Road and the old Royal Mail sorting office in Short Street, where I worked as an auxiliary postman in the early eighties. How did that old postman joke go? 'Not much of a job, but better than walking the streets.'

Some of the finest people I have ever known worked for the Royal Mail. When my colleagues saw me early each morning, sorting the mail for my round, did they suspect that I was the most famous secret agent the world has ever known? It was doubtful.

I handed in my resignation after ten months, concluding that my job at the Post Office was grubby, poorly paid and wholly lacking in prestige. M was disgusted with me. To my father, any job, no matter how humble, was preferable to unemployment. The problem went deeper than that. As Head of the Secret Service, he was probably wondering how I was ever going to protect Western civilisation from communists, terrorists and criminal masterminds when I could barely drag myself out of bed each morning.

It had been hard to see my father in that decaying ward, and harder still to leave him there. Not that his stroke had made any real difference to our relationship. In the past, we had always avoided saying the few things in life worth saying. Nor were we saying them now.

At the same time, M had made it perfectly clear that he valued me. This most undemonstrative of men had implied that I was the best shot in the service. Previously, this fact was only known to M, his Chief of Staff and the Instructor on the shooting range. Plus the millions of people throughout the world who have read *Moonraker*.

Of course, common sense told me that my dad couldn't even talk, let alone send me out to save humanity from the clutches of another criminal mastermind. There hadn't been a decent criminal mastermind since Auric Goldfinger.

It wasn't just the villains who had lost their glory. Since Fleming's death, 007's literary career had taken a nosedive. After Kingsley Amis's creditable stab at his life and times in *Colonel Sun*, the trustees of Fleming's estate hired a writer called John Gardner to keep the dream alive. If you believe Gardner, Bond has cut down on the smoking, drinking and womanising and his eyes are no longer fierce slits. As 007 said in *You Only Live Twice*: 'Balls! And balls again!'

Nobody understood me like Ian Lancaster Fleming. He captured my snobbery, my sensuality and my unique resistance to pain with impeccable attention to detail. Fleming used to maintain that he wrote thrillers for 'warm-blooded heterosexuals'. But for me, at this critical hour, the twelve novels and two short story collections that chronicle the career of James Bond 007 were far more than thrillers. They offered an invaluable refuge from a world I could no longer bear.

At the end of *You Only Live Twice*, Fleming's penultimate book, Bond strangled his arch-enemy, Ernst Stavro Blofeld, with his bare hands. This was perfectly reasonable behaviour on 007's part, as Blofeld had murdered his wife, Teresa, in the previous novel, *On Her Majesty's Secret Service.* During his escape from Blofeld's castle of death, Bond suffered a head-wound that caused serious damage to the temporal lobe of his brain. The result? Total amnesia.

By the time Fleming came to write *The Man With The Golden Gun*, both he and his creation were mere shells of themselves. Fleming was terminally ill with heart disease brought on by smoking and drinking. Bond was a mental wreck. His amnesia had been capitalised on by the Russians, who de-programmed him, convinced him that he'd been working for the wrong side and sent him to England to assassinate M.

Fortunately, Bond's murder attempt failed. M decided to let bygones be bygones and gave him back his double-0 number. I knew from personal experience that one of M's finest qualities was his willingness to forgive and forget, without bearing grudges.

The Bryce family were always short of money, despite the

ludicrously long hours that M worked. Whatever the Ministry of Defence were paying him, it wasn't enough. My brother and I never got a new pair of shoes before we had worn holes in our old ones.

When I was fourteen, I asked for a pair of shoes for my birthday, even though my old ones were only partially worn out. I really wanted to know how it felt to see two pairs of shoes sitting at the bottom of my wardrobe.

Dad gave me some money, and I went to Stockport on the 192 bus, humming the Bond theme all the way. I don't remember how it happened, but on arrival in Stockport, I forgot about shoes altogether and started thinking about records. Not even records that I liked, but records that I hoped would impress Véronique so much that she would agree to have sex with me.

Véronique Gillain was my French penfriend. At my new school, a grammar school, we were expected to put our study of the French language to practical use by corresponding with French children. The arrangement also involved exchange trips, giving English children the opportunity to witness the misery of life in a typical French home, and vice versa.

I have always loved France, ever since studying Longman's Audio-Visual French at school. We would sit in darkened classrooms on hot summer afternoons, watching endless slide shows about the fictional Marsaud family. It was a family of five, not including the dog that was always playing with its ballon. Monsieur et Madame Marsaud, their rather wimpish son Jean-Paul, and two strapping girls called Marie-France and Claudette.

Marie-France was the eldest daughter, with breasts that Ian Fleming would have approved of. In my memory, she still looks like Véronique, the pretty penfriend who made me the envy of my schoolfriends. How proud I had felt when I flew to her maison in Beziers, convinced that I was about to lose my virginity at the age of thirteen.

And what did I find? That Véronique, as tall and exciting as any Bond girl, was a devout Catholic, afraid to remove her brassière in case she went to Hell. Worse still, her family expected me to speak French at all times.

I wasn't interested in the French language at all, unless it was being spoken by a naked French woman. So mealtimes became a thrice-daily, gut-wrenching ordeal. As Véronique's long-faced mere and pere watched in silent disapproval, I would try to ask someone to pass the croissants and never once be understood.

This was nothing to the embarrassment I felt when it was time for my penfriend to visit England. She came from a gleaming middle-class home in a well-heeled suburb, so it tortured and shamed me to introduce this dazzling Gallic beauty to my narrow, unglamorous parents and their un-Bondian semi-detached values. I needn't have worried. Véronique took people as she found them. She left the petit bourgeois snobbery to me.

She adored M, who joked with her, and whom she called 'Papa'. She charmed my mother, who put away her steel-spiked shoes for a week and became hideously ingratiating. My brother also fell in love with her, although he had a peculiar way of showing it. One night, Véronique and I came home early from the youth club to find Richard watching television, dressed in her underwear.

Despite such misadventures, or perhaps because of them, Véronique and I had kept in touch. We had not met since childhood, but had continued to exchange letters, photographs and 'Joyeux Noël' cards. In all the time I had known her, she and I had never done anything more intimate than holding hands. Yet in our hearts, we remained faithful. She would always be my best friend in France.

But I digress. The point I wish to make is that Véronique loved Led Zeppelin and Mike Oldfield, and by her own admission 'all wonderful music'. That was how I came to return home with three albums. The only one that qualified as 'wonderful music' was the original motion picture soundtrack of *On Her Majesty's Secret Service*. The other two were *Tubular Bells* and *Led Zeppelin 2*.

Like Oddjob, M blew a fuse. I don't really blame him. Led Zeppelin were a bloody awful group.

'I gave you money for shoes and you came back with two bloody records,' he spluttered.

'Three records,' I retorted, behaving like a fourteen-year-old.

'Why? Why?' he kept repeating.

To which I replied: 'It's my birthday. Why can't I have what I want?'

M could provide no satisfactory answer to this question, which was a shame. He could have won me over for all eternity by simply telling the truth: 'Because now I have to buy you shoes as well. And I don't earn enough to buy you three records *and* a pair of shoes.'

A day later, we were friends again. By which I mean, we

were able to resume our amicable but not entirely successful relationship. When I played the *OHMSS* soundtrack on our family's humble Fidelity stereo, Dad chuckled warmly and called in my mother. 'Ivy? Come and listen to this.'

As always, she obeyed him. Her only comment was: 'Ooh. Very jazzy.'

M's memory was dire. To him, the music he was hearing was a revelation. Years had passed since he took me to see *OHMSS* at the Davenport cinema. It may have been my second-favourite mission, but to my dad it was just a film. He could not remember who George Lazenby was, or how he, Myles Bryce, a simple working-class man from Salford, had felt when Bond escaped from Piz Gloria on a pair of stolen skis.

But I remembered.

A thin smile of satisfaction had appeared on M's face as the descending chords of the *OHMSS* theme buzzed through the cinema and I stepped into my skis. That smile broadened when my moonlit descent was noticed by the guards, who shouted something that sounded absurdly like: 'Schnell! Der Englander is up der hole!'

When Blofeld, played superbly by Telly Savalas, hurled down his white cat and rushed out to head the pursuit, M sniggered. He was never particularly fond of animals. M laughed again when Blofeld fired a flare, monitored my descent through binoculars and proclaimed: 'We'll head him off at the precipice.' (My father laughed because he knew an ironic reference when he heard one. I didn't see the joke. To me, the line sounded like wonderfully exciting movie dialogue. It still does.)

M moved to the edge of his seat when I lost a ski halfway down, and was forced to mono-ski the rest of the way. 'He's only got one ski,' I gasped. My dad smiled and nodded, glad that I was paying attention.

With a lurch of sadness, I suddenly pictured M sitting in the hospital. Before his stroke, whenever he saw people who were aged and infirm, he used to say: 'It's a bloody shame. I'd rather die than linger on like that poor old bugger.' Knowing that he was now a poor old bugger himself filled me with a dull ache that I could chart with clinical precision. The pain began at the back of my throat and ended in my solar plexus.

I turned off the main road and ambled down Chapel Street to look at my old school. The wrought-iron gates were hung with heavy padlocks. A sign bolted to the railings read HAZEL GROVE COUNTY JUNIOR SCHOOL. I had no idea what the school was like now, but in the 1960s it had been an appalling place. Most of the pupils came from the poorest district of Hazel Grove, a place called the valley where all the children had mean, narrow eyes like John Wayne and wore the same socks all week long.

On my first day at school, a boy from the valley, disliking my clean, polished face, banged my head against a wall until it bled. Then he got frightened and begged me not to tell anyone. Out of some laughably misplaced sense of schoolboy honour, I agreed. I had to have stitches and to wear a bandage around my head, which made me feel heroic.

My parents must have guessed that I hadn't really slipped in the playground. Why didn't they take me out of that dreadful dump there and then? Because it would never have occurred to them that they had any choice in the matter. Like most people of their class and generation, their lack of confidence was equalled only by their blind respect for authority. They probably believed that the state was doing them a favour by educating their children. To quibble about the *quality* of that education would have struck them as downright ungrateful.

The teachers at Chapel Street meted out physical punishment indiscriminately. In this respect, they were worse than the valley kids, who only hit you if you refused to give them money or jammy dodgers. By the time I was eleven I had lost count of the number of times I was slapped, slippered and caned, usually for no crime greater than talking in class. My mother was as bad as the teachers, and there would have been no point in complaining about these daily attacks to M. Although he hit his own children rarely and without conviction, he claimed that corporal punishment was necessary to uphold discipline.

It was worse than that. At parents' evenings, when he met my teachers face to face, M actually used to say: 'If John steps out of line, give him a crack.' As if the bastards needed any encouragement! For years, I mistook his attitude for insensitivity. But what if he was demonstrating uncommon foresight?

For me to be an effective agent, it was essential that I be toughened up at an early age. How else could I have survived the physical hardship that I had been subjected to over the years?

Think about it. In *Casino Royale*, my genitals were thrashed with a carpet beater and a Russian assassin autographed the back of my right hand with a stiletto. In *Live And Let Die*, the little finger of my left hand was bent back until it snapped. I came close to castration in *Goldfinger*. In *Diamonds Are Forever*, I was kicked senseless by two thugs wearing football boots. I actually died in the final chapter of *From Russia With Love*, only to be revived in *Dr No* when Fleming realised that without the Bond novels, he would have nothing to do during his annual two-month vacation in Jamaica. Yes. Maybe there was method in the old man's madness.

Then again, perhaps I was making excuses for him. Perhaps my father endorsed institutionalised violence because he was an unimaginative, forelock-tugging working-class conformist. Not that it made the ghost of a difference to the way I felt about him. Whatever happened, he would always be M and I would always be his finest agent.

When I arrived at Compton Drive, the house was in darkness. I walked round to the back gate. My father's Nissan Bluebird was parked on the drive. I was insured to drive the car and Mum had already mentioned that I could borrow it during M's illness. But to me, it seemed depressingly like an old man's car. In *Moonraker*, Bond 'thrashed' his Bentley down the Dover Road. *Goldfinger* saw him 'flinging' his Aston Martin towards Rochester. But you could thrash and fling the Nissan as much as you liked: it would still be comfortable at sixty, scared at seventy and positively frantic at ninety. If the Bluebird had been issued by Q Branch, my old friend Major Boothroyd would have had one hell of a job selling it to me.

'I must say, 007, that I find this business of equipping you on your mum and dad's drive highly irregular.'

'Where's my Aston Martin?'

'It's had its day, I'm afraid. M's orders. As of now, you're to drive this 1989 Nissan Bluebird saloon with power-assisted steering. M won't be needing it himself, and it's a shame to waste a perfectly good motor car.'

'But it hasn't got any gadgets!'

'Ah, now that's where you're wrong.' Then Q would draw my attention to a small panel of switches in the door. 'This is one innovation that I'm particularly proud of. See? Electric windows, front and back. If anyone leans into the car and starts threatening you, simply press a button and . . . Hey presto! You'll trap their head.'

'Oh, so what? Lots of cars have electric windows. Where are the machine guns? The ejector seat? The bullet-proof shield? I know . . . maybe it converts into a mini-sub like that car in *The Spy Who Loved Me*?'

'Afraid not.'

'Oh, bloody hell!'

'Well, what about this device in the dashboard? It may look like a perfectly ordinary cigarette lighter. But grab a man's finger, push it in here and he'll get a pretty nasty burn.'

'I've got a better idea. Why not ask him politely if he'll lie down in the road for me? Then I can just drive over him.'

'007, you of all people must realise that we don't have an Aston-Martin-kind-of-budget at the Ministry any more. The cold war is over. The device we came up with to overcome your father's speech problem cost the equivalent of the entire budget of *Goldeneye*. Now be a good chap and be grateful for what you've got.'

'So all I get is this heap of junk?'

'No! You get a car that I myself would be proud to drive.'

'Here are the keys. You're welcome to it.'

'Oh, don't be so silly . . .'

'No. I'm serious. I have a licence to kill. And a licence to drive any vehicle. But I'm not driving my dad's car, and that's final.'

Then I would walk away without looking back. Q would remain silent until I reached the corner, then shout: 'Oh, grow up, 007!'

I was back at Great Ormond Street in time for lunch. Tracy was sitting beside James's cot with an open sketch book on her lap. Pale faced, she asked me where I'd been. I told her I'd had a strong feeling that my dad needed me, so had paid him a visit. She took my hand and looked searchingly into my eyes. 'John, you mustn't do things like that to me. You can't go off to buy something and not come back. It isn't fair.'

I shrugged. 'I'm sorry. It was just an impulse.' I handed over a bar of Lindt. 'At least I remembered this.'

'Great. I'm getting so fat that they'll have to build a new wing just to house my arse.'

I looked down at James, reassured by the roundness of his face. 'He's put on weight,' I commented cheerfully.

'He's lost weight,' said Tracy sullenly. 'They're putting him on some new milk to fatten him up.'

I surveyed her artwork. She was drawing a cartoon bird with a large bill and wild spiky plumage. 'What are you doing?'

'Nothing.'

'Come on. What?'

'Oh, I'm sick of just sitting around doing nothing. I'm going to make a patchwork quilt. To give to the hospital.'

'Why?'

'You know, to hang on the wall . . . brighten the place up.' Irritably, she added: 'What do you mean "why"?'

'Just that, well, hadn't we better wait to see what they do for James before we start giving them presents?'

She sighed. 'It isn't just for the staff. It's for the children. And their families.'

Without comment, I picked James up and held him.

'All the families who come here are in pain,' concluded Tracy. 'So that's what I'm doing.'

'Have you settled on any design yet?'

'Give me a fucking chance. I've only just started thinking about it.'

'It's just that I've had an idea,' I said. 'You know the James Bond eye that appears at the start of every Bond film? Well, you could make a quilt based on that. But instead of Bond appearing in the centre of the eye, you could put a baby there.'

Tracy gazed at me for a long time. Then she astonished me by saying: 'John, is there something wrong with you?'

At the time, Tracy's reaction made no sense to me. It took me eight hours to see her point. The 'James Bond eye' was essentially an icon of death. Decorating a hospital with a baby in a blood-red eye would have been a monstrously distasteful act. Better by far to show 007 himself in the eye, his Walther aflame as he shoots directly at the onlooker.

But I didn't bother suggesting this, for fear of alienating her further.

The silence and boredom of the next few days were overwhelming. Endlessly wary of me, Tracy now divided her time between James and the quilt. In Bondian terms, this period of waiting was equivalent to those lengthy plot-exposition sequences that have ruined most of the Bond films. Who wants to watch model spaceships taking off anyway? In *Thunderball*, much of the model work was so clumsy that they ought to have re-named it *Thunderbirds*. Half of *Goldeneye* was devoted to setting up a villainous plot that had already appeared in *Diamonds Are Forever* and was as boring as shit the first time.

Real life, of course, is almost exclusively comprised of boring bits. Assignments don't turn up that often. Fleming's Bond only had two or three missions a year and spent the rest of his time arsing around his Regent's Park office, writing a self-defence manual called *Stay Alive!* But when you've had to see Vulcan bombers, space capsules, helicopters and even nuclear submarines being hijacked in *Thunderball*, *You Only Live Twice*, *Moonraker*, *Goldeneye* and *The Spy Who Loved Me*, a manual called *Stay Awake!* would be far more useful.

When I was young, the lack of 'action/adventure' in the real world became markedly obvious during the school holidays. Whereas Bond, John Steed and even the Famous-bloody-Five scarcely had to walk out of their front doors to have adventures, Hazel Grove was disappointingly free of fiendish adversaries of any description.

As a teenager, this absence of excitement impelled me to manufacture conflict for its own sake. I started picking fights with other boys. If I couldn't find anyone to fight, I would start on Richard, who had the advantage of being younger and weaker. Yet it was Richard who cured me of the desire to inflict pain.

Our last battle had ended with me sitting on Richard's chest, banging his head repeatedly against the garden path. Each time his head hit the concrete, it made a horrible dull clunk. The sound and the impact began to vibrate in my own skull. Suddenly my brother's head became inseparable from my own. His bones were my bones. Overcome by nausea and remorse, I let him go. He demonstrated his profound gratitude by ratting on me to Mum.

Sickened by this incident, I relinquished violence as a means of self-expression. For the remainder of my teens, I immersed myself in poetry, art and music. In the process, I lost interest in James Bond.

It took the baby's birth and these long dreary days in Great Ormond Street for me to realise that, like 007, I was fundamentally a man of war. And nothing made me feel more war-like than sitting beside my son's cot. Although I wanted the best for the baby, he still seemed like a stranger to me. Yet whenever a doctor or nurse made him cry, I wanted to kill them.

One evening, a strange nurse lumbered into Room 4, approached James's cot while he was sleeping and tried to take his pulse. She was a short, dumpy woman with sturdy arms and legs and a flat, wardress face. Her pale blubbery lips were crowned by a nicotine-stained moustache. I couldn't tell what her breasts were like, but it's a safe bet that they were like badly made sandwiches.

On an impulse, I picked up a chair. Holding it by the back, with its legs pointed like horns, I held the old bitch at bay. 'Keep away from the baby,' I warned her. 'And no tricks.' Her yellow eyes narrowed, sizing up the situation. Then she backed away, out of the room.

Tracy went white. 'Great. Well done. Now you've attacked a member of staff.'

'I doubt that very much. Didn't you notice? She was no nurse. That woman didn't know one end of a baby from another. Whoever she was, I must have scared the living daylights out of her . . .'

The next day, Tracy insisted on having breakfast with me. We went down to the Peter Pan café to see what culinary delights were on offer. One of the many things that James Bond and I had in common was that we both liked to start the day with a good breakfast. The woman at the counter seemed to be unaware of this fact. Her only greeting was a surly nod.

'I'd like scambled eggs with two thick slices of whole-wheat toast, followed by a double helping of coffee.'

She shrugged. 'No scrambled eggs.'

'No scrambled eggs?'

'Only fried.'

I grimaced. 'Then fried will have to suffice. How about the double helping of coffee?'

'What you mean "double helping"?' Her unfortunate face and accent betrayed her Eastern European origins. 'Do you mean two cups? I not know what you mean.'

I shuddered. 'Two cups of very strong coffee from De Bry

in New Oxford Street, brewed in an American Chemex. Black and without sugar.'

'We've only got instant. Take it or leave it.'

'What was all that about?' demanded Tracy as she watched me eat.

'You must forgive me,' I said, paraphrasing Bond in *Casino Royale*. 'I'm a bit pernickety about what I eat and drink. It comes from spending so much time alone.'

Calmly, she said: 'Would you like to spend more time alone?'

'What do you mean?'

'Just that you seem very angry at the moment. It's really difficult to deal with, John. Why do you think all the doctors and nurses talk to me rather than you? Because they're scared you're going to knife them or something.'

'I'm not that bad.'

'You fucking are,' she affirmed. 'What about the way you treated that nurse last night? Don't you think she'll have warned everyone about you? They'll have you down in their notes as an OAP.'

'Thirty-seven isn't old.'

'Not that kind of OAP. It's hospital code. It stands for "over-anxious-parent".'

'Anxious? I'm not anxious.'

'Is that all you're going to do? Sit there and contradict everything I fucking well say? Or is there a chance that we might actually have a conversation?'

I knew she was right. We needed to talk. It wasn't as if I needed time to concentrate on my food. I wasn't remotely hungry. 'I just don't want them to do to James what doctors and nurses usually do to patients – to misdiagnose him and kill him. We're placing his life in the hands of complete strangers. Strangers that I don't trust and I don't particularly like. My dad was saying the same thing only last night . . .'

She leaned forward in her seat. 'What did you say?'

'I . . .'

'Are you telling me that M can talk?'

'No. No. But I know how he feels . . .'

'But you said "My dad said the same thing". I heard you.'

'No you didn't.'

Tracy said nothing but her eyes glistened with love and sympathy. 'It's hard, isn't it? James and M being ill at the same time. It's so horrible.' I nodded. 'John. Lovely-face. Listen to me for just a moment.' She placed her hand on my arm. 'I can manage here. I *have* managed. Why don't you go home for a few days. Relax. Get drunk. Watch bloody James Bond videos!'

'But you need me here.'

'No. Not while you're as hyper as this, John. You're too bad-tempered. You're just making a bad situation worse.'

'I don't want to sit at home. That'd be as bad as sitting here.'

'OK. Then go away somewhere. Hire a car and have a break from everything. Why don't you?'

'You're sending me away?'

'No. Yes.'

'I don't believe it.'

'Only for a couple of nights. Just to get yourself together.'

'Who says I'm un-together?' (Tracy gave a guilty shrug.) 'Shit, Tracy. You've been talking about me, haven't you? Talking about me behind my back.'

'Only to Fiona.'

'Who's Fiona?'

'The liaison sister. She's there to help parents with their problems. I told her about you. She says that sometimes it helps if Mum or Dad take a complete rest from hospital routine.'

I snorted rudely. 'Mum or Dad? Is that what the silly cow calls people?'

'Fiona isn't silly.'

'You realise that Fiona was one of the chief villains in *Thunderball*?'

Tracy laughed and shook her head. 'And you don't think you need a rest?'

'Where would I go?'

'You tell me,' said Tracy. She smiled mischievously. 'Where would James Bond go?'

7

His New Incredible Adventures

I cleared French customs as the dusk was settling on a bright, fragrant day in early spring. My mission? To drive around France in the tread-marks of 007, starting at Le Touquet and travelling south-east as far as Moulins, then circling to Paris and the forest of St Germain, ending at the Normandy resort of Deauville, the probable blueprint for Royale-Les-Eaux in the first James Bond novel, *Casino Royale*.

I was driving a brand-new Aston Martin DB7, hired at hideous expense from a garage in Luton. Under my left armpit nestled a Walther PPK in a Berns-Martin triple-draw shoulder holster. Both the gun and the holster were replicas, purchased from a specialist dealer in Camden.

Wearing the weapon did not make me feel foolish. On the contrary, it gave me the same warm sense of security that toy guns had instilled in me as a child. The weight of the holstered gun against my ribs comforted me, as it must have comforted the literary 007, who was nowhere near as tough as Sean Connery.

Connery's Bond overcame Robert Shaw as Red Grant in hand-to-hand combat on screen in *From Russia With Love*. In the book on which the film is based, Bond won't even countenance a fight with such a formidable adversary. Instead, he pretends to be dead so that he can stab Grant in the crotch.

My father seemed to think I was James Bond, licensed to kill. He hadn't made it clear whether I was supposed to be Fleming's Bond or the movie Bond. The cinematic version could beat up everyone apart from Jaws and Oddjob. But in the books, 007 gets a pasting on a regular basis. If I was meant to be Fleming's Bond, I definitely needed a gun because I couldn't even fight as well as Roger Moore.

Now, Roger Moore was not James Bond. Neither was Sean Connery, who once, a little hurtfully, said that anyone who took the Bond films seriously was in need of a psychiatrist.

I wasn't Bond either. I had no illusions on that score. I was John Bryce, licensed to be depressed. But for the next forty-eight hours, I would eat, drink and drive like 007. Whatever M had claimed, I knew that my son's surgeon wasn't a Bond villain. He couldn't be, because real life isn't that interesting. During my journey, perhaps the true nature of my mission would be revealed to me.

Unexpectedly, the DB7 made me nervous. In first gear, I only had to pat the accelerator with my toe for the car to surge forward like a pouncing tiger. If I slipped the gear lever into third like Sean Connery in *Goldfinger* when he was chasing Tilly Masterson through the Alps, not only did the Aston Martin leave all other traffic behind: it left me behind too, waiting in the rain at the 192 bus stop after a Bond film. The DB7 was built for speed. I was built for standing still.

In this respect, I took after my father. M's driving was not fast but safe, law abiding and accident free. His unwillingness to exceed thirty miles an hour used to irritate me, especially if we were driving home after a Bond film. 'Dad? Why don't you drive on the pavement for once? Then the police can chase us and we can make them crash into walls and each other. Why not, Dad?' Curiously, he never answered me.

M always drove the family car. My mother had never shown any interest in driving. Even if she had, it is unlikely that M would have allowed her to drive *his* car. Once, when I was learning to drive, he took me out for a practice session and almost died of heart failure. 'Not left . . . I said right . . . oh, bloody hell! You came within a fraction of hitting that van. A bloody fraction!' Lucky for him that he wasn't sitting beside me when I was tearing round Las Vegas in *Diamonds Are Forever* with the Nevada State Police in hot pursuit.

Dad's motoring was at its absolute slowest when he was driving his family through an unfamiliar holiday resort. At these times, strange, new light poured in through the windscreen. The car cruised past bright holiday shops, beach balls and balloons bobbing under their windows, plastic windmills fluttering madly in the sea wind. Richard and I would sit together on the back seat, fingers crossed, silently praying. 'Please God, don't let the hotel be as bad as last year.' Except that we didn't stay in hotels, only guest houses with a set menu and slightly stained table cloths.

While privately sharing our misgivings, M would strive to

appear nonchalant and in control. I picture him with his exposed elbow resting on the sill of the open window. For his annual holiday, my mother always bought him a couple of cheap serviceable polo shirts. I remember how the sleeves of his T-shirts flapped and swelled as he drove.

On a car journey, M would frequently only half-smoke a cigarette. Then he would tuck the remainder behind his left ear. He referred to these half-fags as 'dimps'. In my memory, he always had a dimp behind his ear by the time we approached our holiday destination.

Fleming's novels fail to make it clear whether James Bond tucked dimps behind his ear or not. On the whole, I find it unlikely. We do know, however, that Bond lit his cigarettes with a black oxidised Ronson lighter. I had purchased such a lighter at the Duty Free shop. Unfortunately, I had been unable to find a gunmetal case to keep my cigarettes in. This was a minor disappointment, no more. A double 'O' agent does not rely on props, but on his own native daring and tenacity.

I lit another cigarette and tried my best to inhale. Bored of Consulate, I had bought a packet of Gitanes. When in France, die as the French die! The smoke rasped harshly in the back of my throat and tasted vile. In a hundred years, I reflected, tobacco would be obsolete, along with nuclear power, petrol and television game shows. For the time being, James Bond smoked, and I had chosen to live like James Bond. So I had no bloody choice!

Until his triple-bypass operation, my father smoked like a beagle, remaining loyal to Players, the brand that had been steadily destroying his respiratory system since the war. 'Players

Please' went the slogan, which must be up there with the advertising greats like 'I'd love a Babycham' and '*Dr No*, the first James Bond film!'

The Players packet bore a picture of a bearded sailor with the word 'Hero' on his cap. In the novel of *Thunderball*, Domino spends four boring pages describing how this sailor was the first real love of her life. Personally, I always thought he looked like a raving homosexual.

The miserably small boot contained a suitcase that was not much larger than the case Tilly Masterson used for her rifle in *Goldfinger*. Into this case, I had crammed clothes, toiletries, and the four Ian Fleming books that featured France: *Casino Royale*, *On Her Majesty's Secret Service*, *For Your Eyes Only* and *Goldfinger*. On the vacant seat beside me rested my cigarettes and lighter, a Michelin guide and a CD called *The Best Of Bond*, an anthology of all the Bond themes from *Dr No* to *Licence To Kill*. Now, as I approached Étaples, I experienced a sudden craving for this music.

Then I learned something else about the DB7. Not only was it short of missiles, machine guns, armoured glass, oil slicks, smoke screens, showers of metal spikes, high-powered jets of water, lasers in the hub caps and a bullet-proof shield: it didn't even boast a CD player. The car stereo played cassettes only. Once again, I was reduced to humming my theme tune. Not that I cared.

As I drove, the DB7 clinging to the bends with a grace and ease that my father's Nissan Bluebird would not have been capable of, I felt rejuvenated. There was a hint of ruthlessness to my mouth and my blue-grey eyes were hard and alert. Like 007, I was never happier than when I was on the job.

This time, I was not on the trail of Mr Goldfinger, who in any case, was throttled in the final chapter of the seventh James Bond novel. Instead, I was searching for the man I knew myself to be.

Before leaving England, I had phoned Véronique. She was delighted to hear from me. We had arranged to rendezvous in Paris, where she worked at a bank on the Rue de Rivoli. Not only did I have an Aston Martin and a toy gun: tomorrow I was destined to have lunch with the most beautiful Bond girl in France.

'James Bond is back in action!' the movie poster for *Goldfinger* had announced. 'Everything he touches turns to excitement!' How apt those words sounded to me now. Nearly as apt as the slogan for *OHMSS*: 'Far up! Far out! Far more!' Although my personal vote went to *Thunderball* for: 'Look up! Look down! Look out!' To this, one might easily add: 'Look daft!'

My first port of call was one of Bond's favourite French restaurants, 'a modest establishment, unpromisingly placed exactly opposite the railway station of Étaples'.

According to Fleming, the restaurant concerned was owned by a Monsieur Bécaud. In *OHMSS*, 007 sojourned there to consume Turbot poché, sauce mousseline, and half the best roast partridge he had eaten in his life, washed down by half a bottle of Mouton Rothschild '53 and a glass of ten-year-old Calvados with his three cups of coffee.

The only hostelry in approximately the right location was called Mon Plaisir. I sat down at a table by the window with

OHMSS open for reference in front of me. But when I enquired after the health of Monsieur Bécaud, the pretty waitress started giggling. In retaliation, my features relapsed into a taciturn mask, ironical, brutal, and cold. I ordered Turbot poche, but was duly informed that the poche was off.

By way of compromise, I settled for oeufs cocotte. Fleming maintained that scrambled eggs were best seasoned with finely chopped chives or fines herbes and served on hot buttered toast in individual copper dishes. I didn't bother passing these specifications on to the chef. The French are notoriously touchy about these matters, and I didn't fancy eating eggs that had been liberally laced with Gallic spit. The food was accompanied by a bottle of Dom Pérignon '64: a vintage year for champagne, Bond films (*Goldfinger*) and novels (*You Only Live Twice*) but a terrible year for Ian Fleming, who died that August.

I 'ate steadily and with absorption'. The scrambled eggs were excellent. Probably. Personally, I can't stand scrambled eggs. With my coffee, I smoked another Gitane, made especially for me by Gitane, the Gitane people. I was too excited to care about the meal. I could barely believe that I was really in France, by myself, with an Aston Martin parked outside.

When I was a child, my family never went 'abroad'. My first excursion out of the country was a school trip to Switzerland, when I was twelve. I was filled with a religious awe when I first saw the Matterhorn and stood rigidly to attention while the boys around me argued and farted. I loved Switzerland, which is probably why the alpine scenes in *Goldfinger* and *OHMSS* still strike such a John Barry chord in me.

Throughout my entire childhood, M was not tempted to

leave the country. On family holidays, we never travelled further than Torquay. I used to think we couldn't afford to go 'abroad' but have since reached the conclusion that M simply wasn't that keen on foreigners, with the exception of my penfriend Véronique and every foreigner he had ever met.

In the last two weeks of August, M saw more of Richard and me than in all the other weeks of the year put together. He wasn't always impressed by what he saw. Once, when we were playing football with M on the beach, a boy of my age ran up and joined in our game without being asked.

Richard and I resented the intrusion. Because our quality time with M was strictly rationed, we were unwilling to share him. But M was raised in the Salford slums, where one ball was shared among twenty children and street games were a riotous free-for-all. He was happy to let any child play with us.

The boy was slightly pompous, or so it seemed to Richard and me. In a confident Home Counties accent, he said: 'Give me lots of headers, 'cause headers is what I need.' This made my brother and I snigger. M glowered at us but made no comment.

Months later, when Richard and I were laughing at a man on TV for having an indecipherable regional accent, M suddenly turned on us and said, with fiery contempt: 'You're just a couple of snobs. You were the same with that lad on holiday. Snobs! You make me sick, the pair of you . . .'

Then I angered him further by pointing out that the boy on the beach had been far posher than any of us. M shook his head and walked out of the room. Like Anita Ekberg on the billboard in *From Russia With Love*, I 'should have kept my mouth shut'.

My father had a point. As a boy, I was a dreadful snob. When I first saw *The Avengers*, I was as besotted by Diana Rigg's rich Home Counties voice as by her face. It made no difference that she was raised in Doncaster, and had learned to speak that way at RADA. Her voice ravished me. My parents could not open their mouths without advertising their lack of education and their working-class origins. M, in particular, was proud to be ordinary.

Once, when I needed a new pen for school, M reluctantly took me to a newsagent. 'What kind of pen would sir be thinking of?' mused the shop assistant obsequiously. 'The cheapest,' answered M with a bitter little laugh.

My parents called me 'the duke' because at every opportunity I wore sunglasses and a blue corduroy jacket with epaulettes. I asked for the jacket for Christmas. Mum made it at home on her sewing machine. Whenever I wore that jacket, I sincerely believed that I was the most stylish ten-year-old on the planet.

I now accept that I must have looked quite ridiculous. But it didn't matter that other kids smirked, or that a grown man on the seafront at Blackpool pointed me out to his girlfriend and said: 'Look at that twat.' In my heart, I knew that if Diana Rigg had seen me in my corduroy jacket with epaulettes, she would have adopted me on the spot. Although I doubt Sean Connery would have been impressed. Come to think of it, it was probably Connery who called me a twat.

Tragically, Diana and I never met. She and I were kept apart by our positions in life. We had different friends and interests. We seldom dined in the same restaurants. My family didn't dine out at all, unless Mum had forgotten to make the sandwiches on a day out to Fleetwood.

Then we would sit in a crowded, smoky café, eating chips with mushy peas. Eating in public mortified my father. If Richard and I started telling jokes in a café, M would always silence us with a red-faced 'Enough!' or 'Just calm it!' He honestly seemed to think that there was something ill-mannered about laughing or even talking at the dinner table. God knows what he'd have thought had he walked into Simpsons or The Ivy any lunchtime, to see table-loads of rich, over-fed businessmen laughing their silken socks off.

During our 'proper' holidays, our annual family fortnight by the sea, Mum avoided the shame of cafés by buying fruit, sausage rolls and doughnuts so that we could picnic on the beach. Sand always got into the food and the fizzy drinks were never served below the temperature of 38 degrees fahrenheit. This used to annoy me. When James Bond had a picnic by the Thames in *From Russia With Love*, he took the trouble to chill the champagne in the river. If Steed and Mrs Peel had a picnic, they usually had a Fortnum and Mason's hamper. They didn't have to drink warm Coke or eat gritty doughnuts out of brown paper bags.

On holiday mornings, M used to rise early, then wash, shave and dress before strolling down the promenade to buy *The Daily Express*. Occasionally, Richard or I would accompany him, the smell of toast and bacon drifting up to us as we descended the stairs of the guest house. If he met any fellow guests, M barked out 'Good morning' in a stiff, oddly formal voice, afraid that his true manner of speech would betray the fact that he didn't consider himself rich enough to stay in a crappy guest house.

M's social awkwardness dismayed me. In bars, I wanted him to snap his fingers and say: 'Waitress, a large gin and tonic with one whole lime. Cut the lime in two, squeeze the halves into the glass, pile in crushed ice and then pour in the tonic.' But all he ever said was: 'A pint of your best bitter. Please, love. When you've got a moment . . .'

If a meal isn't prepared properly, I will always send it back, again and again, until the bastards get it right. M hated complaining, always preferring to suffer in silence. It would have embarrassed him to tell people that their food, drink, manners and service stank, so he either said nothing or pretended to be satisfied.

During a restaurant meal with my wife and my parents, M broke out into a cold sweat when Tracy, a vegetarian, sent back a mushroom omelette because it contained shreds of ham. 'Can't you just pick the ham out?' he urged her. Mystified, she said: 'Why would I want to do that? Why can't I have what I ordered?' M did not answer. Under that gruff, frosty sailor's exterior, my dad lived in a state of permanent anxiety.

I asked for the bill and went to the washroom to splash cold water on my cold, taciturn face. As I was walking back to my table, something fell to the bare wooden floorboards with a resounding 'clunk'. I looked down and saw that my Walther had fallen out of its holster.

Before I had time to retrieve the weapon, the pretty waitress stooped down and passed the Walther to me. She was smiling. 'Pour votre fils?'

'That's right,' I said, my eyes glittering dangerously. 'Everything I do is for my son.'

I left the waitress a substantial tip. At the door I turned and made her laugh again by saying: 'Don't forget to write.' Then I walked out into the mild evening, regretting that I hadn't plucked up the courage to invite the waitress for a spin in my Aston Martin. But I quickly reminded myself that on a job, women got in the way. When they weren't in bed with me, they were either working for the opposition or getting themselves covered from head to toe in gold paint.

Like 007 in *Goldfinger*, I covered the next 43 kilometres in fifteen minutes. Now, some thirty-eight years after Bond pursued Goldfinger's Silver Ghost down the N1 to Abbeville, the road was still 'badly cambered'. After all that champagne, I was feeling badly cambered myself. Outside Chartres, I pulled into a lay-by for an un-Bondian snooze.

Fleming was rather rude about Orleans. He called it a 'priest- and myth-ridden town without charm or gaiety'. 007 stayed in the Hôtel de la Gare while shadowing Goldfinger, but the Hôtel de la Gare had vanished. I opted for Le Rivage, a modest hotel to the north of the city that overlooks the Loire. The Loire was Bond's 'favourite river in the world'.

An elderly porter took my minute suitcase from the DB7's boot. At reception. I half-expected to be greeted by a fawning manager: 'Ah! Mr Bond. You will be requiring your usual suite?' Then I remembered that 007's international fame was a conceit created in the Bond films, underlined by that terrible moment in *Diamonds Are Forever* when Tiffany finds Bond's wallet on the corpse of Peter Franks, turns to Sean Connery and says: 'My God! You've just killed James Bond!'

Suddenly, even third-rate diamond smugglers had heard of 007. No agent had ever been less secret. But the young receptionist on the desk, although clearly aware that I was a 'handsome bastard' had never seen me before in her life. This anonymity suited me. I didn't want everyone knowing my double-0 business. I signed the register 'John Bryce'. Then I followed the doddering porter up in the lift to my room with a view of the glittering river.

Once I was alone, I undressed. I took a long hot bath followed by an ice-cold shower. Then, naked except for a shoulder holster, I practised a few quick draws in the mirror. Satisfied that my eyes were looking sufficiently blue-grey, ironical and cold, I dressed for dinner. But before leaving my room, I removed a few blue-black hairs and with the aid of saliva, glued them over my drawers, case and wardrobe door because I'd seen Sean Connery do this in *Dr No*. Ian Fleming had Bond do the same thing in *Casino Royale* and *OHMSS*.

In the restaurant, I ordered a dry martini. But not just *any* dry martini.

'Served in a deep champagne goblet.'

'Mais oui, Monsieur.'

'Listen carefully. I want you to get this right. Three measures of Gordon's, one of vodka, half a measure of Kina Lillet. Shake it vigorously until it's ice cold, then serve with a large thin slice of lemon-peel. How does that sound?'

'Utterly crap, Monsieur.'

Bond called this concoction 'The Vesper' after Vesper Lynd,

the heroine of the first 007 novel, whose grave he visited once a year. When my drink arrived, it tasted so bitter that I shuddered. None the less, I swallowed it and immediately ordered a second. I was curious to see how two vodka martinis would affect me on an empty stomach.

In no time at all, I was as pissed as a newt. Perspiring slightly, I ate one of Bond's favourite meals: a 'large sole meuniere and an adequate camembert'. Then I drank a well-iced pint of Rosé d'Anjou and had a Hennessy's Three Star with my coffee. Feeling dizzy and slightly sick, I left the restaurant, checked that no one had etched 'James Bond is a sissy' into the paintwork of my car, and attempted to refresh myself by taking an unsteady walk along the tree-lined river.

What was my mission called, I wondered? As a boy, the titles of Fleming's books often thrilled me more than the stories themselves. My three favourite Fleming titles, *Live And Let Die*, *On Her Majesty's Secret Service* and *You Only Live Twice*, all played on popular expressions. When I was ten, I used to lie awake at night trying to think of similar titles for the Bond novels I was surely destined to write. Thus the sequel to *To Guard A Living Target* became *Death Is For Dying*, my memorably incompetent inversion of the well-known saying 'Life is for living.'

On returning to my room, I satisfied myself that no one had been through my belongings. The tell-tale hairs were still in place. I undressed and took a cold shower. Then I brushed my teeth and 'climbed with relief between the harsh French sheets'. I lay awake for a long time, listening to the hotel plumbing and the doors opening and closing all around me, suddenly aching to see Tracy and the baby again.

In *Moonraker*, Fleming wrote that marriage and babies were 'out of the question' for double-0 agents. The implication being that a commitment to the living made an agent considerably more reluctant to risk death. I had heard professional soldiers say the same thing. Once you had a wife and children to love, throwing yourself into the path of a bullet started to seem wasteful, stupid and futile. You would never, ever, mean as much to the army or for that matter, the Secret Service, as you meant to those who loved you.

Then I remembered that James Bond was also a father. At the end of *You Only Live Twice*, Kissy Suzuki is expecting his child. Bond, who is suffering from amnesia, never learns about Kissy's pregnancy and at the end of the book, leaves her in order to appear in his next adventure, *The Man With The Golden Gun*.

If James Bond had come face to face with his child, it's a safe bet that he would have been as bemused by the experience as I was. It's not as if 007 has little nephews or nieces to practise on. Bond has no family, and few friends. His only responsibility is to himself. Even his unflagging pursuit of personal gratification is officially sanctioned by his employers. Why get serious with women when you could get killed at any moment? It was the ethos of RAF fighter pilots in the war. Eat, drink and be ruthless, for tomorrow you die. *'For Tomorrow, You Die'*. Now, there was a Bond title that I would have killed for when I was ten years old.

At least 007 had a reasonable excuse for shirking the responsibilities of parenthood. My reasons were as shallow as Ian Fleming's, who, in keeping with upper-class tradition, studiously avoided any strenuous or meaningful involvement in the rearing of his only son. I may have favoured mineral water over Fleming's 'serious drinks' and preferred reflective solitude to the arse-licking and the social-climbing that he went in for. But we were both essentially self-obsessed men who didn't want our cosy lives to be disrupted.

Some fathers adored their children as soon as they were born. I had met such men, seen them changing nappies with what Fleming would have described as 'alarming alacrity' and entering into the spirit of parenthood with delighted and delightful zest. But I was always a late starter, in life, in love, even in espionage. It took me a long time to accept and adapt to change. And as far as changes go, becoming a parent was still fairly cataclysmic.

And what did I feel for my son now, as I lay hundreds of miles away from him in this soft, well-sprung French bed? I felt curiosity. Were his eyes as large, dark and all-encompassing as I remembered? Were his hands and feet as tiny and as perfect? I had developed an *interest* in him. Nothing more, nothing less. But that was still an advance on the eerie detachment I felt before. 'Any advance on eerie detachment? Going once! Going twice! One late-twentieth century male infant! Sold to Mr John Bryce of Chelsea in Fulham!'

Tracy would have loved this hotel. We had never stayed anywhere so grand. She thrived on room service and crisp white sheets, but we could only afford modest holidays. Throughout our marriage, money had been a permanent worry.

How sweet it would have been to escape hospitals and insane, patronising doctors for good and to have Tracy and the baby here with me now, not worrying about money or missions.

Thinking only of love. Fleming called it the 'soft life'. He said that 007 feared soft living more than he feared death. My God, I could have done with some of that softness now.

I suddenly felt moisture on my cheeks and wondered where it had come from. I eased myself out of bed, walked into the bathroom and turned on the light. Strange! There were droplets of water on my face. While I was drying myself with a fresh towel, I realised that I needed a pee. One of the most far-fetched aspects of the Bond films and books is that although 007 drinks inordinate amounts, he never seems to empty his bladder. In *The Living Daylights*, he actually locks himself into a lavatory cubicle, yet still isn't tempted.

But as I turned to do what James Bond had never done, it struck me that in a Bond film, this would have been the perfect moment to find a familiar figure sitting on the lavatory. A tall thin man with a mop of straw-coloured hair, sharp, hawk-like features and a steel hook where his right arm used to be. He would be wearing a tan-coloured lightweight suit and when he smiled, deep laughter lines would appear at the corners of his grey eyes. The stranger was smiling now.

'Felix Leiter! What the hell are you doing here?'

'I would have thought that was dam' obvious. Now how's about some privacy, Commander?'

'No dice. Not until you tell me why you're here.'

'Does there have to be a reason? Hell, you know as well as I do that even when you're on a mission in America, you seem to do all the work and the CIA just stand around looking like middle-aged bit-part actors.'

'I can't argue with that.'

'The truth is, maybe this time I have a darned good reason for being here. In fact, it's a honey. I'm worried about you, old buddy.'

'Why?'

'Because you don't seem able to live in the present, James. You only seem to feel things in retrospect. It takes a near-fatal stroke to make you realise you love your old man. Get a grip on yourself, feller. What's it going to take before you realise you love your kid?'

'Do you have any children?'

'Nix!'

'Nix? What the hell is that supposed to mean?'

'Search me. I was kinda hoping you'd know. Ian Fleming makes me say it in the books, anyway. Guess it must have been something Americans said in the fifties. Anyways, just think about what I'm saying.'

'Which is?'

'That so far, you've only been half-awake and half-alive. But it's possible to be happy now, to live and feel *now*. To be alive and fully conscious in the right-here-and-now.'

'Go on. I'm listening.'

'Sorry, 007. That's it. I'm a minor character, remember. I never get enough lines. And that's the end of my scene.'

8

His New Incredible Enemies

I awoke at seven, not looking forward to breakfast or yet another cold shower. But, as Fleming never grew tired of mentioning, breakfast was Bond's favourite meal of the day. Manfully, I ordered double helpings of coffee and orange juice and two fresh, speckled brown eggs laid by French Marans hens. I ate out on the balcony, breathing in the scent of the river. The eggs were followed by two thick slices of wholewheat toast, spread with the hotel's own fine Apple Marmalade. I drank my coffee black, without sugar. Then I smoked a cool reflective cigarette; coolly reflecting that if this was how Ian Fleming really lived, it was no wonder that he died of heart disease at the age of fifty-six.

In *Casino Royale*, Bond is said to smoke seventy cigarettes a day. By *Thunderball*, he's cut down to sixty. As Bond's personal habits, prejudices and rather saturnine good looks were inherited from his creator, it's a safe bet that Ian Fleming got through three or four packs of high-tar Morland specials a day and at least half a bottle of vodka or gin.

This would be in addition to his daily consumption of champagne or claret, which Fleming didn't regard as 'serious drinks'. Fleming's idea of a serious drink was half a tumbler of hard liquor, diluted with ice, lemon and a shot of vermouth or tonic water.

Ian Fleming drank at lunchtime and in the evening. His idea of 'evening' might be any time between five and six p.m., depending on how bored he was feeling. During his annual two months in Jamaica, he went swimming at least once a day. Apart from that, despite being a gifted athlete as a schoolboy, he took no exercise. Hardly surprising, then, that by the time he was fifty, he had a purple face and an arse as wide as the satellite dish in *Goldeneye*.

The author passed his inglorious regime onto 007, allowing wishful-thinking to play a part in the process. When Bond is subjected to a medical in *Thunderball*, the only side-effects of his hedonistic lifestyle turn out to be slightly raised blood pressure and a furred tongue. In the year that *Thunderball* was published, Fleming suffered a heart attack from which his health would never recover, partly because Fleming refused to cut down on his drinking and smoking.

The only person I'd known who was as wilfully self-destructive as Ian Fleming was my Uncle Len. Len was M's brother, rarely to be seen without a 'ciggy' hanging from his mouth. He smoked Senior Service, which like Players, were untipped. His house was full of huge cavernous ashtrays, stolen from various public houses. Over the years, Len's advanced tobacco habit had stained his fingers the colour of café au lait.

I loved Len. He was cheerful, rude and touchingly child-like. His fascination with America and the Wild West meant that he drove old Cadillacs and sometimes visited our house wearing a large white stetson. Long before I dreamed of spying for England, I shared Len's desire to be a cowboy. My uncle's favourite TV programmes were *Wagon Train*, *Maverick* and *Gun Smoke*, all of which I dimly remember. Like the gunslingers he admired, Len was fond of a shot of whisky.

Although younger than M, Len's excesses ensured that he beat my father onto the operating table for a triple bypass operation by three years, followed eight years later by a stroke that mirrored my father's in every respect. But while the only two words my father could say were 'are you', the two words that remained to Len were rather more useful. They were 'sod' and 'off'.

It was profoundly satisfying to visit Len in hospital and see him responding to every patronising consultant or junior bungler in the same blunt way. 'Hello, Mr Bryce. How are we feeling today?' 'Sod off.' 'Did you have your physio this morning?' 'Sod off.' Len didn't realise that he was being insulting. He imagined that he was saying: 'Yes, Doctor' and 'Thanks for all your help, Doctor.'

Len recovered sufficiently to be capable of driving a specially adapted car. He also regained the full use of his small but ingeniously abusive vocabulary. Yet after surviving a major stroke, Len disappointed his doctors and his family by doing an 'Ian Fleming'. His remaining years were devoted to serious drinking.

After Uncle Len's funeral, my father, who had often

expressed mild disapproval of his feckless younger brother, rested his forehead against the steering wheel of his car and sobbed. Until that moment, I had never seen my dad cry.

These depressing memories now actually gave me strength. The two brothers had similar constitutions and had been disabled in exactly the same way. And if boozy, chain-smoking Len could recover some movement and most of his speech, then so could my moderate, sensible father.

The climb-back wouldn't be easy. M was proud, thus guaranteed to detest being pushed about in a wheelchair. Particularly by my ill-coordinated mother, who would undoubtedly crash him into walls and lamp posts and then blame the wheelchair for having 'funny wheels'. But there was hope for M. Real hope. If James Bond could whizz down Piz Gloria on one ski, my father could fight his way back to health with one arm.

I spent the morning 'motoring comfortably along the Loire'. This would have been a timely moment to be overtaken by a spirited single woman driving a Triumph or a Lancia Flaminia Zagato Spyder, a scarf tied round her hair, 'leaving a brief pink tail that the wind blew horizontal behind her'. Unfortunately, there's never a pink tail around when you need one.

Disheartened, I joined the A71 at Bourges and headed back towards Paris, where I found myself ridiculously early for my rendezvous with Véronique. It was not yet noon. I parked the Aston Martin near the Champs-Elysées and went for a nonchalant stroll. Shortly, I came across a cinema that was showing *Goldeneye* with subtitles. Why not? Why the hell not?

I bought a ticket for the film and a grand café au lait. The film was just beginning. It was the unlikely moment in the stylish main titles where a gun emerges from a woman's mouth. I sipped my coffee and watched Pierce Brosnan's performance with fresh sympathy, feeling that he exuded good humour and charm. He wasn't as good as Sean Connery. But nobody is – including Sean Connery.

If I'd grown up with Pierce Brosnan as James Bond, I'm sure that Connery would have seemed coarse and excessively hairy by comparison. There was no doubt that Brosnan could act, and he certainly appealed to the two young women sitting behind me in the cinema, who kept sighing girlishly during his close-ups.

Pleased with the way my film career was progressing, I stepped out into the bright sunshine and walked to Fouquet's for my first drink of the day. According to Fleming, cafés were not for serious drinkers. At a French café, one was only offered 'musical comedy drinks'. In this situation, I always had the same thing – an Americano. (Bitter Campari, Cinzano, a large slice of lemon peel and soda.) For the soda Fleming always stipulated Perrier, claiming that good soda water was the cheapest way to improve a mediocre drink.

John Bryce was never much of a drinker, 'serious' or otherwise. But James Bond never did anything in moderation, so I sat outside on a pavement table and 'downed' two Americanos. They tasted bloody awful, to be honest. So did the Laurens Jaune that I smoked after it.

Impatient to see Véronique again, I glanced up and down the busy street, despairing of the roaring traffic just as I did in *From A View To A Kill*, a short story in the *For Your Eyes Only* collection. A young couple were arguing at a neighbouring table. The woman was quietly annoyed, but her boyfriend looked furious. He was waving his arms about wildly and shouting. Then, with shocking violence, he grabbed her by the hair and yanked her head down sharply, forcing her face to collide with the surface of their table.

She tried to break free, but he caught her, dragged her to her feet and rammed her forcibly against the window of the café. I was always a sucker for a damsel in distress – most of us so-called tough guys are. Like me, the other patrons had watched the nasty little drama unfold and were gasping in dismay and sympathy. None of them was willing to intervene. It was a job for 007. Unfortunately, 007 was a fictional character.

I rushed over and stood beside the couple, slightly disconcerted by the size of the young man. He was taller than me and appeared to be twice as wide, with enormous hands. Those hands were now clasped around his girlfriend's throat. On her forehead, she had a bruise as big as an avocado. He spoke to her softly, viciously, dominating her with his eyes. It was clearly a relationship made in hell.

Annoyed that my grasp of the French language was so basic, I reached into my jacket and produced a pocket-sized French phrasebook that I'd picked up at Le Touquet. Eventually I found a word that would suffice. 'Arrêtez!' I cried. The young man turned, dismissed me with a glance and a rapid mouthful of Gallic abuse, then returned his attention to his girlfriend. The young woman looked at me, injecting urgency into her eyes. But it was impossible to say whether the look was a warning or an appeal for help.

I looked through the phrasebook again, eventually finding the words I wanted. 'Bâtard! Lâché!' I shouted, which meant 'Bastard! Coward!' I also wanted to call him a big ugly girl, but he lunged at me before I could locate the appropriate phrase.

'Hector!' yelled his girlfriend, throwing herself between us. I don't know why, but unpleasant and worthless men frequently have stupid names. 'Hector, non!' she screamed. I translated this as: 'No, Hector! Kindly desist, Hector!'

I reached for my Walther. Perhaps staring down a gun barrel might bring the brute to his senses. But my shoulder holster was empty. I'd dropped my bloody gun again. So as Hector hurled his girlfriend to one side and came for me, massive arms flailing, I was obliged to engage in hand-to-hand combat. To his surprise and mine, I blocked every blow that he threw at me. I think his girlfriend was surprised, too. For a while, she even stopped shouting: 'Hector!'

He eventually gave up trying to hit me and did his best to strangle me. The power in those hands was frightening. I clasped my hands together as if praying and jerked them up between his massive wrists. Then I flung open my arms to break his grip and punched him in the face as hard as I could.

He stepped back, astonished. But instead of falling unconscious to the ground like the minor Bond villain he undoubtedly was, he retaliated with renewed force. He managed to hit me twice, in the mouth and on the chin. It was the first time I had ever been punched by a grown man. Previous to Hector, the only punches I recalled receiving were delivered by little boys in the school playground. Those blows may have stung, but they were nothing compared to the mighty, brain-shaking wallops that I was experiencing now.

Soon, Hector and I were rolling in the gutter. His girlfriend started shouting: 'Hector, non!' I found myself thinking: 'This joker weighs a ton. If he sits on me, I'm finished.' When the police arrived to break up the party, I was heartily relieved.

Hector and his girlfriend were interviewed by three strapping gendarmes. I was quizzed by a smaller officer who spoke English. He quizzed me sympathetically. Then asked if I wanted horrible Hector to be charged with assault, warning me that Hector's girlfriend had already accused me of interfering.

I shook my head. Wasting my time on such a trivial affair would make me the laughing stock of the intelligence community. The gendarme looked relieved, happy to be spared the paperwork. Before we parted, he leaned towards me and said: 'If it is any consolation, you have given him a beautiful black eye. Bonjour. Thank you.'

Badly shaken, I returned to my table. No one acknowledged me. I could taste blood. I looked down and noticed my Walther on the floor beside my chair. Not caring who saw me, I picked up the gun and rammed it back into its holster.

I felt foolish and ashamed. Hector's girlfriend, like Teresa in *OHMSS*, was 'a bird with a wing down'. It was bad enough that I had failed to punish Hector. Tonight, he would probably beat up his girlfriend twice to make up for this afternoon's abortive attempt. Worse than this was the knowledge that the girl resented my intrusion; that in her eyes, Hector had more right to hurt her than I had to help her.

My mother used to accuse the Bond films of being 'far-fetched'. But what could be more far-fetched than the world we live in, where villains walk free and are worshipped by those they betray?

As I contemplated this bitter fact, one of the most beautiful women I have ever seen in my life walked up to my table. She was tall, with long light brown hair. She was shaped like Ursula Andress in *Dr No*; sturdy but feminine, full-figured without being fat.

She had long, tanned legs and like Vesper in *Casino Royale*, she was dressed in a black dress that was simple but elegant. Her mouth was wide, generous and full. Her cheekbones were high. Her eyes were not grey but an astonishingly piercing shade of green.

'Véronique?'

'John? But you've grown so big.'

'You too.'

She eyed me dubiously. 'I've only just arrived and you're insulting me already!'

'Not at all. You look absolutely stunning.'

I hugged her and was about to say: 'The name's Bond. James Bond,' when one of my front teeth dropped out.

'Shit,' I said, holding the fallen incisor in the palm of my hand.

Véronique held her hand to her mouth to stifle a laugh, then apologised for laughing. 'Oh no. This is horrible. I make your teeth fall out.'

I called a waiter over and in an unattractive lisp, ordered a drink for Véronique. She asked for a diet Coke with ice. While we were waiting, I explained that I'd been in a fight. She was appalled. 'So this man knocked your tooth out?'

'Not exactly,' I lisped. 'It's a capped tooth. He must have dislodged the cement. I just need to get it glued back on.'

'Well, look,' she said decisively. 'A friend of mine is a dentist. He works just round the corner from here. Let me take you to him.'

'But I've booked a table at that restaurant in the Eiffel Tower where they filmed scenes for *A View To A Kill*.'

'No, no. We're having lunch at my place. I want you to meet Gaby.' Gaby or Gabriel was her three-year-old-son, the beloved souvenir of a failed marriage. 'First, we must get that tooth fixed.'

We walked away, forgetting to pay for my drinks or the Coke I'd just ordered. No one came after us. This seemed apposite. In the Bond films, 007 never seems to pay for anything. At the most, he slips the doorman a few quid on his way out of the casino.

Chatting happily, Véronique led me down the Champs Elysées. We turned into a little tree-lined avenue and stopped outside a discreet office block with business plaques lining the entrance.

This was where her friend the dentist held surgery. His name was Philippe, a small, plump, unassuming man wearing colossal bifocals. Philippe reattached my tooth free of charge and advised me to floss more regularly.

Back on the street, I asked Véronique what Philippe meant to her. 'Oh, he's just a friend.'

'I'm glad to hear it.'

She smirked knowingly. 'Don't be so obvious.'

Rewording a great line from *Thunderball*, I replied: 'When you've got as little time as we have, you have to be obvious.'

She laughed. 'Hey. You're married.' She paused and clutched my arm. 'And yes! I nearly forgot! Thanks for the photos you sent of James and Tracy. He is so beautiful, your boy. He looks just like Tracy, in small!'

Feeling that it would be criminal to correct a linguistic error as charming as this, I said: 'Lucky for him.'

'Oh. I don't mean . . . you are nice too.'

'I may not be the Elephant man,' I conceded. 'But I can't compete with Tracy. Or you, if it comes that.'

She laughed delightedly. Véronique had been an exuberant teenager. It was strange and delightful to see that same vibrant, questing energy embodied in a grown woman. Arm in arm, we wandered down to the river.

She took a packet of Gauloises from her bag and offered one to me. I accepted. We lit our cigarettes from the same flame. I gazed into her eyes and felt dizzy. It was like being thirteen all over again.

She noticed the way I was staring at her and tossed her hair back provocatively. 'Anyway, what about your baby? Do you like him?'

Seriously, I said: 'Yes. I do.'

'Little boys are lovely. The best. And he's healthy? No problems?'

'None.'

'That's good. You know, it can be hard if a new baby is not well. Gabriel had jaundice. Am I saying it right? Jaun-dice? When he was born, he needed to be kept under a special light. It was so worrying.'

Desperate to change the subject, I said: 'I've got some more photos to show you.'

She dismissed the idea airily. 'I'll see them later. We have all night.'

I stopped and looked at her. 'We don't, you know.'

Disappointment filled her face. 'Why not?'

'I'm going to Deauville tonight. I've got to go to the casino.'

'Why?'

'It's just something I need to do.'

'Can't you cancel?'

I sighed. 'No. It's work. Look, why don't you come with me? I've got a suite at Le Royal. There's probably room for two people.'

She sighed. 'I can't. I can't leave Gabriel. It's the nanny's night off.'

'Then bring him with you.'

'I can't, John. I've got work tomorrow.' She glanced at her watch. 'Let's go back and get something to eat. I thought we had more time. Merde!'

Disheartened, we walked to the Aston Martin in silence.

Then we drove across town, through heavy traffic. She was delighted by the car. 'John. When did you buy this? It's a James Bond car!'

'Not exactly,' I confessed. 'Bond drives a DB5 in *Goldfinger* and *Thunderball*. In *OHMSS*, he's switched to an Aston Martin DBS. Then there are all those soppy cars that Roger Moore drives, until Tim Dalton gets behind the wheel of an Aston Martin Volante in *The Living Daylights*. Suddenly, in *Goldeneye*, Pierce Brosnan is driving a DB5 again. But this is a DB7. So you see . . .'

I gave up. Véronique had started laughing after my opening sentence and was now wiping tears from her eyes. 'Stop. You are *too* funny. Making all those names up like that . . .'

Her small but luxurious flat was situated in the exclusive Reuil-Malmaison district. When we arrived back, her son Gabriel was sitting with the young Finnish nanny, watching a cartoon show on TV. He was a quiet, fair-haired three-year-old with his mother's extraordinary eyes. When Véronique stooped to kiss him, he barely reacted. Adoration was nothing new to him.

Introducing me to the nanny, Véronique said: 'Hannele, this is John, a very good friend of mine. He's actually the real James Bond.'

Hannele laughed. In clear and careful English, she said: 'Yes. I already thought there is a resemblance.'

'I need a drink,' said Véronique, taking off her coat and throwing it over a chair. She went out to the kitchen and returned with three glasses and a bottle of Bollinger. Addressing the nanny, she said: 'Hannele, won't you join us?'

We drank a toast, firstly to our children, then to any children the nanny might produce on her return to Finland. Of his own volition, Gabriel walked across the room and embraced my legs. The pleasure of being touched by him passed through me like a mild electric shock. 'Papa,' he said. Then, grinning, he pointed up at me. 'Papa.'

For two full seconds, I saw what I'd been missing, glimpsed how thrilling and fulfilling fatherhood might be. Then the amnesia that I suffered at the end of *You Only Live Twice* returned to swamp me and the moment was lost.

The two women made suitably womanly noises. Although I knew that Véronique was estranged from her husband, I had no idea how often, if ever, Gabriel saw his father. Véronique crouched down and spoke softly to her son in French.

I hauled off my jacket rather too quickly. My wallet, keys and cigarettes flew across the room. I stopped to reclaim my belongings, then realised the room had gone strangely silent.

I looked up. Hannele was staring at my chest fearfully as if the tarantula from *Dr No* was squatting there. Véronique looked stunned, as her gaze switched from my face to the Walther in its shoulder holster, then back to my face again.

Her mouth opened in dismay. 'My God, John. What is this?'

Véronique pretended to accept my hastily concocted explanation: that I was wearing the gun to win a bet. But when I tried to remove the Walther from its holster to prove that it was a fake, the two women almost had hysterics. 'No. Non!' insisted Véronique. 'Not in front of Gabriel!'

I hastily put my jacket on. But the damage had been done. For the remainder of the afternoon, Véronique's eyes exhibited unease and mistrust. As I was leaving, my best friend in France begged me to tell her what was wrong. It would have been the perfect opportunity to talk to her about James, my father and how everything in my world was dragging me down. I simply shook my head and drove away.

It was late afternoon when I arrived at the sedate Normandy resort of Deauville. I checked into the imposing Le Royal and went up to my luxurious suite overlooking the sea. I ordered two vodka martinis from room service, and drank them quickly while I was unpacking.

Then, as the sun was setting, I put on my leather jacket as worn by Timothy Dalton in *The Living Daylights* and walked down to the beach. There was hardly anyone in sight. A cold wind blew across the channel, whipping the waves into a white-edged frenzy. I was grateful for the warmth of my jacket.

It was impossible to stand beside the sea and not think of M. Ian Fleming pressured his employer at *The Sunday Times* to give him two months' paid leave at the start of each year. My dad's employer obliged him to take two weeks' paid leave at the end of August, the busiest and least desirable fortnight of the season. As a result, the holiday beaches that Richard and I played on as childen were ludicrously crowded.

Tonight, like James Bond, I would try my luck at the gaming tables. By rights, M should have been here to give me money to gamble with. M approved of gambling, in moderation. For the rest of the year, M was a skinflint. But when we went to Goodrington Sands near Torquay, he used to give Richard and me vast amounts of cash to squander in the amusement arcades. I was always a natural gambler, which is why the casino scene is a staple ingredient of any Bond film or novel.

Like most gamblers, Richard and I devised a foolproof system which we adhered to slavishly. Our method was as follows: we entered the amusement arcade and inserted every coin we had into the slot machines. Any money that we won would be disposed of in the same fashion. As soon as we were penniless, we would return to M and ask him for more coins. Without argument, he would reach into his pockets and fill our palms with change. Then we would return to the amusement arcade to put our foolproof system into action once more.

On holiday, M seemed to have an infinite amount of change. His pockets chinked as he walked. For the rest of the year, M drove. He only seemed to walk on holiday. When he strolled along the promenade, arm-in-arm with my mother, he employed a peculiar stiff-legged gait that was supposed to appear casual but merely looked self-conscious. Dad found it impossible to relax.

On particularly hot days, M would sometimes be moved to wear his swimming trunks. It was only then that Richard and I got to see his battle scars. My father got shot in the war. The bullet pierced his abdomen, missing his vital organs and exiting via his back. It happened when he was in the RAF, stationed in Burma. What an Admiral in the Royal Navy was doing as a private in the Air Force is beyond me. Perhaps M needed a change.

M claimed that his wound ached whenever it was about to rain. I don't know whether this was true or not. He refused to be drawn into any discussion about his wartime experiences, and stoically resisted any attempts by old comrades to 'get back in touch'. I suspect that M had a bad time in the war and saw lots of sad and ugly things that he didn't care to be reminded of.

As a boy, none of this mattered to me. I was simply thrilled to have a father who was wounded in action. One of my schoolfriends, Roger Jowett, was actually jealous. 'You lucky git, Bryce,' he used to say. 'My dad's never been shot by anyone.'

Sometimes in the mellow holiday evenings, M ambled off on his own, soon returning with tickets for some unappetising seaside show. The headline acts at these shows were usually lack-lustre British acts that had risen to prominence in the fifties and sixties, only to end up at the end of the pier in the seventies. People like Kathy Kirby, Norman Vaughan and The Bachelors. Even their names depressed me.

I don't know why, but I invariably sat next to M at these seaside shows. Needless to say, it was quite a different experience from watching a Bond film with him. There were no women in bikinis – at least, none under the age of fifty. M didn't laugh and neither did I. While the headline acts recycled their tired old routines, my attention wandered and I found myself staring up at my dad, thinking how indescribably awful it was that one day this kind and decent man would cease to be alive.

Not once did it occur to me that everyone in the theatre was going to die, or indeed, that the performers on the stage were dying at that very moment. I never transferred my pity to Mum or Richard or myself. I reserved my boyish compassion for my father, because he was so much older than me and old people have an unfortunate habit of expiring just when you love them most.

I couldn't tell M what I was feeling there and then, not while he was listening to The Bachelors. There is a limit to the amount of torture a man can stand. And afterwards, eating chips and hot dogs while we idled back to the guest house, my attack of melancholy began to seem self-indulgent and faintly ridiculous. Yes, M would die one day. So what? Hopefully, The Bachelors would beat him to it.

Now, I bitterly regret that I was unable to tell my father something so important. He may have eyed me coldly and said: 'Stuff and blithering nonsense! What d'you think this is? The women's institute? If you can't conduct yourself properly, like an English gentleman who's repressed his distress and can't express what he hasn't repressed, then I'll get 008 to replace you.'

But in his heart, I'm sure M would have been absolutely thrilled. After all, I would have been telling him that I didn't want him to die, not now, not ever. What else could this have possibly meant but: 'Dad, I've just realised that I love you and you're incredibly important to me.'

On other days, M's death seemed a welcome prospect. There were times when I could have killed him myself. In particular, I'm thinking of one hot holiday afternoon when

Mum went into Torquay to buy a dress and Dad took Richard and me to watch a game of cricket. Or rather, M took Richard and himself to watch cricket and I tagged along because the only alternative would have involved shopping with Rosa Klebb.

At the cricket match, M fell asleep in a deckchair. Richard wandered off alone in his usual unfriendly way, and I was left watching my father's face change colour in the sun. When he turned lobster red, I decided that he was cooked and tried to wake him. I prodded his shoulder. No response. Then I tapped him gently on the cheek.

M awoke with a start, opened his eyes and astonished me by whacking me across the face with all of his strength, which admittedly wasn't much. But the blow was hard enough to make my ears ring. Perhaps my father thought I'd been slapping him for my own idle amusement, rather than attempting to save him from sunstroke. I don't know. No accusations were made, no excuses given. We both remained silent. Fighting back the tears, I stared at M reproachfully and he stared angrily back. I wandered off and found my brother, who couldn't work out why I was so pleased to see him. I didn't tell Richard what Dad had done. I was a secret agent, and my life depended on pretending that nothing could hurt me.

Richard was bored by the cricket, too. He gave me an absurd running commentary on the match. 'And the bowler has just thrown a googly. Or was it one of his goolies?' I laughed hysterically, struggling to bury the pain of what had happened.

I was fourteen years old and had just realised that my father wasn't magical and superhuman; that like anyone else, he could be petty, irrational, even callous. This revelation was partly a relief, because it meant that I didn't have to care about him so much.

The unjust slap on the head forced me to face an important truth. I had grown up thinking of M as my protector, my special friend. Now I had to accept that he was more like a gentle prison warder who wished me well but could only feed me scraps when no one was looking. M didn't understand me but, unlike my mother, refused to condemn me. Yet M adored my mother, and would only defend me from her when her behaviour was at its most unjust. For the greater part of my childhood, I was alone.

I returned to my hotel room, lay down on the bed and lost consciousness. On waking, I threw off my clothes, had a hot bath followed by an ice-cold shower, performed three handstands, then had a hot shower followed by an ice-cold bath. But I still felt tired and bloated. After only thirty-six hours of 007's life-style, I felt in chronic need of the health farm he was sent to in *Thunderball*.

I dressed for dinner, donning a black tuxedo, my elusive Walther taped securely into its shoulder holster with some sticking plaster which I obtained from room service. Then I went down to claim my table in the L'Etrier dining room. From a surly, self-important waiter, I ordered the meal that Bond shared with Vesper Lynd in *Casino Royale*: caviare with plenty of hot toast, followed by a small tournedos, underdone, with sauce Béarnaise and a coeur d'artichaut, ending, oddly, with an avocado pear. This was accompanied by a bottle of Blanc de Blanc Brut. (All together now: 'Probably the finest champagne in the world'.) While awaiting the food, I ordered a small carafe of ice-cold vodka.

The waiters arrived with the caviare, and a mountain of hot toast. This came with finely chopped onion and grated hard-boiled egg. It was all well prepared and faintly disgusting. If this was really the kind of food that James Bond enjoyed, he clearly had no taste whatsoever.

As I mounted the steps to the casino, dark doubts began to assail me. What if admission was restricted to members only? If so, it was highly likely that the casino staff would throw me out on my ear. But the attendant at the door to the salle privée did not ask for my membership card. Instead, he bowed obsequiously and waved me past.

I lit a cigarette and walked slowly through the high-ceilinged, panelled room. The tables were filling up. The scent of Chanel competed with the acrid stench of expensive cigars. Then I approached the baccarat table.

The scene before me resembled a Satanic forgery of Da Vinci's *Last Supper*, with the banker, like Christ, occupying the heart of the table. If I was not mistaken, the Banker was Turkish. I knew this because he was little, neat and ugly with hard, untrusting, bright, angry, cruel and jealous eyes. This, regrettably, is how Ian Fleming describes the 'modern Turks' in *From Russia With Love*.

The Turk before me would only have looked 'modern' in

1968. He was wearing a paisley cravat under a pink shirt. His full lips formed a fixed, almost benevolent smile. On the green baize before him lay the reason for that smile: a mound of gleaming white plaques. He was evidently enjoying a winning streak.

As I approached the table, the chair directly opposite the Turk was vacated by a little old lady who was sobbing passionately into a white lace handkerchief. I glared at the Turk icily. Not content with being hard, untrusting etc he had added 'unscrupulous' to the list by swindling an elderly woman out of her life savings.

The banker whispered something in the croupier's ear. Then, addressing the table, the croupier announced: 'Un banco de cinquante millions.'

The other players at the table gasped, and with good reason. Unless I was much mistaken, fifty million francs was approximately equivalent to five million pounds. Tracy and I had about seven thousand pounds in a high interest savings account, which amounted to our entire fortune. But neither our poverty, nor the very real possibility that the casino would refuse me credit, could prevent me from uttering that magical word, 'Banco.'

The smile on the Turk's lips faded as he raised his face to scrutinise me. At the same moment, I slipped into the vacant chair and blew a great pointless cloud of tobacco smoke across the table, just like Sean Connery in the famous gambling scene of *Dr No*. When the smoke cleared, the Turk was still staring at me. His expression showed polite curiosity, nothing more.

The table fell silent. Still watching me, the Turk eased

four cards out of the shoe. Using a wooden spatula, the croupier deftly flicked two of the cards across the table to me. I glanced at them briefly: the ace of hearts and the ten of diamonds. It was a winning hand!

But only at pontoon.

Sadly, I was playing baccarat. I hadn't the faintest idea how to play baccarat. I'd always skipped the card scenes in Fleming's books, impatient to get back to the sex and violence. Fortunately, baccarat is explained in detail in *Casino Royale* and I happened to have a copy of this book in my inside pocket. I took my 1963 Pan paperback of Ian Fleming's first novel out of my jacket and turned to page sixty-eight.

I was just getting to an interesting bit when the huissier tapped me on the shoulder. His pale face was earnest and apologetic. His breath stank of garlic. 'Mais Monsieur, c'est impossible!'

I eyed him coldly. 'Do you mind? I'm trying to read.'

The huissier grasped my arm. 'Non! It is rude to read at the table.'

'You sound just like my mother.'

His eyes implored me. 'Monsieur?'

I looked up at the Turk. Was there the ghost of a smirk on that dark, ugly, neat face? I emitted a mild sigh. None the wiser about baccarat, I put the book away.

'Well?' said the Turk softly.

'Well what?'

'Do you want another card or not?'

I took a leisurely drag of my cigarette. 'What do you advise?'

The croupier tutted in disdain. The Turk rolled his eyes for the benefit of the other players. In a broad Australian accent, he said: 'I'm the bank, mate. I'm not in the business of giving bloody advice.'

'Some banks are,' I reminded him. 'Lloyds are particularly keen on giving guidance to small investors.'

'What is this bloke on about?' spat the Turk.

'Shh!' hissed the huissier.

I shrugged. 'A card, then.'

Spectators were starting to drift over to the table. Word had circulated that a lunatic Englishman had just accepted a bet of fifty million francs. Nonchalantly, the Turkish Australian flipped over his own cards. The king and queen of spades. Damn! Looked like a pretty impressive hand. Then he passed me my third card, face upwards so everyone at the table could laugh at it. The eight of bloody diamonds. I felt weak with disappointment.

The Turk slipped another card out of the shoe and placed it beside his others. It was no better than my card. The eight of clubs. Was it a draw? Then the Turk started to smile with jubilation and relief. That smile effectively annihilated all of my hopes.

I cursed myself silently. If only I'd researched those Fleming gambling scenes more thoroughly. No matter. Once they'd thrown me in a prison cell, I would have plenty of time to find out where I'd gone wrong. Assuming, of course, that the French prison library had an English copy of *Casino Royale*.

In a sonorous voice, the croupier said: 'Huit à la banque.'

Then he turned over my cards. The unhelpful ace and the

laughable ten. I was about to make a run for it when the crowd around the table cheered. The Turk looked pretty sick.

'Et le neuf!' cried the croupier, raking the Turk's entire fortune over to my side of the table. I laughed in astonishment. In one unbelievable coup, I'd cleaned out the banker and ended the game. And I still didn't know how or why.

The Turk was as amazed as I was. Ignominious defeat was a completely new experience for him. In a voice that was breathless with suppressed rage, he said: 'May I ask who I've had the pleasure of playing with?'

I answered him with the words that I had waited a weary lifetime to say. 'The name's Bond. James Bond.'

After my victory at the tables, I returned to my room. I hung up my dinner jacket. Next, I stood a chair and a card table up against the wall by the door. Then I sat on the chair with my back to the wall and the table to my right. I had loosened my tie and I was wearing my shoulder holster, but my gun rested on the card table. To pass the time, I played Patience with a pack of cards that the hotel had provided. It was exactly like *Dr No*!

But I didn't know how to play Patience, any more than I knew how to play baccarat. So I just laid the cards out in rows and moved them around a bit as the mood took me. This is how I remained, with the door unlocked and the lights turned down low, until there came a soft knock at the door.

I waited. After a short silence, the knock sounded again. Then I heard a voice. A woman's voice. 'John?' I recognised the speaker immediately. It was Véronique.

Not wishing to alarm her afresh, I rushed into the bedroom, took off my gun and holster and hung them in the wardrobe. Then I hurried to the door and let her in.

She was wearing jeans and a black sweater that caused her green eyes to ignite. 'I had to come,' she said simply, throwing her arms around me.

Roger Moore would have responded to this with something crude like: 'Don't we all, darling.' But Roger Moore was merely an actor with a large bottom. I held her tightly. 'Who's looking after Gaby?'

She smiled. 'My sister.'

She drew back from me, her expression earnest. Then she held out her right hand. 'John, what's this?'

In the palm of her hand rested a card covered in transparent plastic. It bore the printed logo of a mother embracing a baby. It was my security pass from Great Ormond Street. It had obviously fallen out of my jacket in Véronique's flat.

'"John Bryce . . . Resident Parent",' she intoned slowly. 'Tell me what this means.'

I had already lied to Véronique once today. I had no wish to lie again. 'It means my son's in hospital.'

I told her everything. All that I felt and didn't feel. I also told her that I didn't believe the baby was ill.

She found this last revelation so bizarre that she asked me to repeat it. 'Your baby has been seen by doctors in this famous hospital, and you still can't believe them?'

'No,' I said wearily.

She took my face in both of her hands and stared earnestly into my eyes. 'John, listen to me. I am your friend and I love you but what you're doing is crazy. Crazy! You can't leave Tracy to face this thing alone. She loves you and needs you. Both of them, they need you so much. Please. You must go home now.'

9

The Man With The Golden Pen

I was back at Great Ormond Street by nine the following morning. Tracy wept when she saw me. I had anticipated anger or one of her marathon silences. Instead she clung to me fiercely in the middle of the Bonham Carter ward and said: 'I thought something terrible had happened to you.'

This struck me as such a ridiculous notion that I laughed aloud. Nothing really bad had happened to me since *Casino Royale*, when the evil Le Chiffre had attacked my genitals with a carpet beater. And in most of my cinematic outings since the sixties, my ability to escape danger has become so pronounced that the films are almost entirely lacking in suspense. I said: 'Darling Tracy, what on earth made you think that?'

'Because . . . because . . .' I waited patiently. When Tracy was upset, it took her ages to tell me anything. 'Because you went away without telling me where you'd gone. You didn't even leave your mobile turned on. What was I supposed to think?'

'But you told me to go. You didn't say anything about ringing you.'

Her eyes darkened with rage. 'I shouldn't have to tell you to pick up a fucking phone. Should I? Or are you so far gone that you've forgotten what you once felt for me?'

Like Tilly Masterson in *Goldfinger*, Tracy was at her most beautiful when she was angry. 'I love you,' I told her.

'Yeah. It looks like it.'

'No. I really do love you.'

'No.' She folded her arms and hung her head, looking touchingly like a sixth former arguing with her boyfriend outside the school gates. 'You think I've ruined your life. You didn't want James in the first place. And now he's ill, you want him even less.'

'Tracy, that isn't true.' She half-smiled and sobbed, wanting passionately to believe me. 'I may not have wanted him before he was born. But I don't wish him away. I want him to be well.'

'But you don't love him. Do you?'

'That's not fair.' I struggled to say the right thing. 'I don't know whether I love him or not. I feel he's part of me. I feel if he died, part of me would die. Won't that do for now?'

She nodded. I put my arm around her and led her into Room 4. James was awake, placidly sucking the nose of a purple hippo, a present from some pop star who had visited the ward in my absence. 'Except that he isn't going to die. Because he isn't ill, Tracy. You do realise that, don't you?'

I saw her wilt inwardly. 'John . . .'

What would Bond have said to convince her? Quoting some lines from *OHMSS*, I said: 'Tracy, I was always taught that mistakes should be remedied. Especially between friends . . . or lovers.'

She groaned. 'Not this again. Have you heard yourself lately? You sound like someone in a film. A *really crap* film.'

Ignoring her completely unprovoked attack on George Lazenby, I persevered: 'Now, listen Tracy. I'm trying to save the baby's life. I know you don't believe me, but you're just going to have to take my word for it. We'd better get a move on. Pack some clean clothes. We have to get away from here. I've got people looking for me.'

I dearly wanted Tracy to say: 'What do they want?' Therefore providing me with the perfect cue to utter Lazenby's finest line: 'I expect they're trying to kill me.'

But she simply stared at me. Then gently, rather *too* gently, she stroked my face. 'I'm not being funny, but listen. Darling, listen. Why don't you have a little sleep and I'll sort everything out.'

'Tracy, I'm not going to lie down quietly while you get me certified.' I stepped out of her grasp and scooped the baby out of his cot. 'Time to leave.'

'Stop it.' Gently, Tracy tried to take the baby from me. 'John, please.'

Before our polite tug of war had time to turn into an unruly squabble, the door to the corridor opened and three men walked in. One of them was Dr Mervyn. The second was a rotund man in his thirties who I hadn't seen before. The last to enter was Emil Shatterheart, wielder of the deadliest scalpel in the world.

Shatterheart straightened his tie and gave me a cautious smile. 'Ah. Mr Bryce?'

I was dumbfounded by his arrogance. The man was acting as if he was a distinguished surgeon and I was a mere parent.

Shatterheart offered me his hand while his minions smiled

ingratiatingly. 'I have spoken to your wife, but not to you. She tells me that, well, we both think that you might be in some confusion about your son's condition.'

I turned to Tracy. She looked away, embarrassed. First she'd confided in the liaison sister, now Shatterheart himself. Was she a double agent, just like Vesper Lynd in *Casino Royale*?

'Hmm.' Shatterheart tilted his head and peered at me dubiously. 'Perhaps it'd help if you told me what *you* thought was wrong with him. That way, we can compare notes.'

I said nothing, merely subjected Shatterheart to my most menacing stare.

Disturbed by the frosty reception, Dr Mervyn took a few steps backwards and studied the floor, pretending to be elsewhere. The other man emitted a high, nervous cough. 'All right,' announced Shatterheart with aplomb. 'We'll leave you in peace. But please: if you have any questions, or any problems that I could possibly resolve, please don't hesitate to contact me.' They left the room hurriedly, pursued by Tracy. Through the glass in the door, I saw her apologising on my behalf.

I could not hear Shatterheart's reply, but the way that he shook his head and patted her arm gave me the general idea: 'Please. Don't worry. Your husband is clearly under a great deal of stress. None of us can predict how the illness of a loved one will affect us. And when that loved one is a child . . .'

I immediately felt ashamed. What the hell did I know? This was the finest children's hospital in the world, staffed by physicians of the highest calibre. If they said James was ill, who was I to argue? It was their word against mine. Not even my word, but my father's. And my father had no words left, apart from 'are' and 'you'!

So I walked out into the corridor to apologise. Tracy broke off in mid-sentence and looked at me in horror, terrified that I might be about to unleash another volley of double-0 nonsense. I allayed her fears by saying: 'Gentlemen, I have every confidence in you. Please feel free to call at any time.'

My attempt to break the ice failed. Shatterheart walked away without answering and the two other men promptly followed him. Dr Mervyn turned to wink at Tracy in an overtly 'matey' manner and said: 'So we'll discuss it today, hmm? I'll fill you in on the details this evening . . .'

'Yes, I'll make sure the kettle's on,' I shouted after him, but he didn't seem to hear.

Tracy concentrated on her patchwork quilt for the remainder of the day, which relieved me greatly. Had she truly gone over to the other side, she would have concealed her contempt for my conspiracy theories and pretended to agree with me.

In the late afternoon, my wife went for a walk around the gleaming corridors. In her absence, a beautiful young dark-haired nurse I hadn't seen before entered and asked to examine James. I permitted this, watching carefully to ensure that the nurse didn't do anything underhand.

Like James Bond, my approach to most women was a combination of taciturnity and passion. But the nurse gave me a smile of such devastating warmth that I felt a slight stiffness coming on. But where to take her? Rome was unfashionable at this time of year, Paris and Madrid too crushingly obvious. No. The ideal venue for our candlelit dinner for two would surely be the Five Ways shopping arcade in Hazel Grove, near Stockport.

After vodka martinis at the Fiveways Hotel, I would lead

her over the road to the Summer Palace restaurant, where an obsequious waiter would escort us to our favourite window table with a view of the busy A523. Then we would order champagne and caviare, with hardly any toast (I always find the problem with really good caviare is that one can never afford enough of it to cover a slice of toast).

After this, the affair would follow its usual pattern: kind words, the touch of a hand, the first kiss, then a longer more passionate kiss. Next we would stay the night at her flat, then my flat. Two weeks of abandoned bliss would culminate in our first weekend away. Monte Carlo? 'So handy for the Rainiers . . .'

All would run smoothly until the fatal argument in a taxi, followed by bitter tears and recriminations, mostly from the taxi-driver. Then more bed, then less bed, until finally I was hiding from her under the bed. One last weekend of torture by the sea would only serve to remind me that I should never have asked her out in the first place.

Bearing all this in mind, I decided not to bother.

When the nurse had left the room, I picked up a grim-looking booklet called 'Cardiac Wing: Parents' information.' This manual provided me with a number of interesting facts. For example, I learned that the Richard Bonham Carter Ward was named after the first paediatric cardiologist in the hospital. Also, that during open-heart surgery, the heart's action is stopped. A bypass machine then pumps oxygenated blood around the body while the operation is carried out on the unbeating heart.

I pictured Shatterheart bending over my son in the operating theatre, and once again, my stomach heaved with fear and distrust. Dr No himself might have been clutching and wringing my innards with his cold metal claws.

At the end of the day, Dr Mervyn returned to Room 4 to tell us what the doctors and the surgeons had decided to do to our son. I was on my knees at the time, struggling to find Channel 4 on the portable TV. Mervyn demonstrated his humanity, if not his competence, by crouching down beside me and gamely trying to help. But he made matters worse. By the time he'd finished, we had BBC2 on every channel.

For a moment I thought that I'd won Dr Mervyn over, that our mutual failure to locate Channel 4 had forged an eternal bond between us. But when he started talking about James, he still persisted in directing most of his remarks at Tracy. He was evidently impressed by how much she knew about the baby. From birth onwards, Tracy had kept a diary, recording each day of our son's young life with meticulous attention to detail.

So when Mervyn asked how much weight James had gained since his admission to hospital, Tracy was able to consult the diary and answer, with absolute certainty: 'Seven grammes, Doctor,' creating the impression that she knew everything about James and that I knew next to nothing. An impression which was wholly accurate, but depressing none the less. Whereas if Dr Mervyn had wanted to know the number plate of Bond's Aston Martin DB5, I could have answered, with absolute conviction: 'BMT 216A.'

Satisfied that James was finally making progress, Mervyn outlined the details of the proposed operation. 'The idea is to graft a patch of tissue over the hole in his heart. Our main worry is that the left ventricle is small compared to the right, and won't be able to cope with the increased flow of blood when we patch up the hole.'

I suddenly noticed that Mervyn's face was incredibly grey. The good cheer he'd demonstrated three days ago had disappeared. He seemed sad and drained, as if too many children had died that day and he was finding it hard to cope. What a curse, I thought, to do a job like his and to care so desperately about your patients. Better to say 'live and let die'.

'Now, listen, you guys,' he said gently, gazing down at the shiny knees of his grey flannel trousers. 'We're talking about major heart surgery, here. It's risky enough for a strong adult, but for a small baby, the risks are obviously far greater.'

I said: 'How much greater?'

I thought, now I have you, my friend. Now you've got to bloody acknowledge me. And what did he do? He turned to Tracy as if she'd asked the question. 'About a one-in-ten chance,' he told her.

Tracy said: 'Of the operation not being a success, you mean?'

'No,' explained Mervyn carefully. 'A one-in-ten chance that he won't survive the operation.' Stunned, Tracy and I looked at each other. Despite the heat, we both shivered. 'It's serious,' confirmed Mervyn. 'I can't pretend that it isn't.'

I said: 'What if you patch up the hole and his right ventricle can't cope?'

Mervyn turned his head and was about to look at me, when Tracy interrupted. 'He means the left ventricle.'

Mervyn returned his attention to her. 'Yes. I know. Well, if that should happen, we'd make a hole in the patch that'll act like a safety valve. He'd be no better or worse off than he is now. Then, at a later date, we'd try something else. We'd possibly give him a Norwood.'

'What?' I laughed. 'You'll give him a motorbike?' The joke fell as flat as a Timothy Dalton one-liner.

Mervyn grimaced, but still didn't look at me. 'You're thinking of a *Norton*. No, a Norwood is a heart op; a two-chamber repair. A pretty drastic re-plumbing job that bypasses the left ventricle completely.' He held up his hands in protest. 'But whoa, now. We're jumping the gun a bit, here. It might not come to that. Let's take things one step at a time, hmm?'

Tracy was close to tears, not eager to hear any more but unable to suppress her agonised curiosity. 'If you put a patch on his heart and all goes well, what are his chances of being able to lead a normal life?'

Dr Mervyn gave her a fatherly smile. 'It's a little early to say, really. No two children are alike. He might only need one operation and grow up to be strong and healthy.'

The dismay on Tracy's face gave way to despair. 'What? You mean he might need more than one operation?'

Dr Mervyn patted her hand. 'We really don't know. Whatever happens, he'll be treated here. His operation will be performed by Mr Shatterheart. I shouldn't really say this, but the man's quite brilliant, he's the best we've got.' He patted James on the arm. 'This little chap couldn't be in better hands, believe me.'

There followed a silence as deep as the hush that fills the cinema when Bond is widowed at the end of *OHMSS*.

'When's the operation going to be?' said Tracy.

Dr Mervyn consulted a small notebook. 'Let's see . . . I've got it written down somewhere . . . I know it's after Easter. That's right. We've pencilled him in for next Tuesday.'

My mouth went dry. A mere four days away.

'It's not definite?' pressed Tracy.

'We'd only cancel your son's operation if we had an emergency.'

'Isn't James an emergency, then?' asked Tracy.

Mervyn smiled benignly. 'Not yet he isn't. Now, try not to worry.' He stifled a yawn. 'Any more questions?' (*Yes. Can you guarantee a live baby, or our money back?*)

Mervyn left us to visit some other grief-stricken, bewildered family. Tracy listened to the sound of his footsteps until they'd faded away. Then she threw her arms around me and wept as if her heart would break.

I held her tight and hummed 'For Your Eyes Only' to her. I asked her if she wanted anything. But she only wanted to cry. She cried until she was exhausted, then fell asleep.

Weary of the hospital, I went outside to sit in my hired DB7, now realising that it was due back on the day of the operation. My trip to France had left the upholstery in rather a sorry state. On the front passenger seat, under the Best of Bond CD and my Michelin guide, I came across a slender file, bearing the words FOR YOUR EYES ONLY.

Of course! This was the dossier on Shatterheart that M had given to me at the close of our last meeting. But as Fleming rightly pointed out, paperwork bored me. The document had been left unopened and unread. Yet now, having failed totally to discover what my assignment was about, I was curious to know what the official file had to tell me.

I lit a cigarette and opened the dossier. With mild surprise, I realised that I was not looking at a file on Emil Shatterheart at all. It was a blank sheet of notepaper with 'Art 'n' Design' printed at the top. Beside these words was a quaint little logo of a paintbrush and an artist's pallette. 'Art 'n' Design' was the name of the firm that my father devoted his life to, the company that chewed him up, spat him out and then went bust anyway.

The notepaper, like the paper that M stole from work for me to turn into James Bond novels, stank of printing ink. Sometimes M took Richard and me to visit the draughty, damp, mouse-infested mausoleum where he worked. You could almost smell redundancy in the air. We were allowed to inspect work in progress, which consisted largely of movie posters for use at cinemas. But never a Bond poster. How could that be?

Before Christmas, there were posters for pantomimes that featured crude caricatures of obscure comedians with red noses and jutting chins. 'Al Read Stars in Mother Goose!' Who was Al Read? And who the hell was Mother Goose?

Sometimes we met M's apprentices; bony-faced teenagers who weren't much taller than me. M was always incredibly kind to them, laughing indulgently at their lamest jokes. Laughing uproariously when they said something pathetically ordinary like: 'Howdy Doody' or 'You're the boss, Myles.' Richard and I were always bemused by this, unable to comprehend why M was never as friendly or cheerful with his own sons.

How mirth-filled our home life would have been if M had found Richard and me as amusing as his apprentices. When he was slumped in his chair, withdrawn and sulking after another day of angry creditors and no fresh orders, it would have been nice to cheer him up with a simple 'Howdy Doody'. Then, while Dad was rolling about on the floor, laughing and clutching his sides, Richard could have finished him off with a well-timed 'You're the boss, Dad'.

It was the same if one of M's bloody apprentices played a musical instrument. 'You should hear young Colin on that guitar,' M would tell us over dinner, chuckling warmly at his mental picture of the amazing Colin. 'He can't play at all, but you know, he's a really smashing lad.' Richard and I both owned guitars. We couldn't play either. But somehow, this didn't make us 'smashing lads', just annoying bastards who made a horrible noise in their bedrooms. 'Turn down that bloody racket. I won't ask you again . . .'

M did his best. I didn't really blame him. I knew that his job had sucked him dry, leaving his family with an ill and weary shell of a man. Losing that job must have crucified him. On M's last day, his beloved apprentices, smashing lads all, had a whip-round and presented him with a gold-plated ballpoint pen, presumably for use while writing his suicide note.

I'm sure M felt that he had wasted his life. So it seemed doubly odd that my father had given me a blank sheet of paper bearing the name of a company that he could no longer bear to hear spoken.

I began to imagine how the document would have read if my stricken dad had been capable of holding his golden ballpoint. He would surely have written to me about his grandson.

* * *

From Stockport With Love

name: James Myles Bryce.

sex: Male.

aliases: Baby James, Cuddly-face, Darling One, Cutie.

origin: A lazy afternoon of uninhibited and wilfully unprotected love-making between John and Teresa Bryce, henceforth referred to herein as 'the parents'.

age: About three months.

description: Height 52 centimetres. Weight 3.310 kilos. Head circumference 35 centimetres. Eyes grey-blue. Hair black. Small, rather ruthless mouth. Languages: none. Smiles infrequently. Does not laugh.

personal habits: The subject's interest in women, particularly in their nipples, is suggestive of a strongly oral personality. Fine gambler. Drinks milk, but not to excess. Does not smoke. Sleeps every four hours.

comment: Promises to be a useful and formidable agent. But his tendency to defecate into his nappy, if not checked, may prove to be a major security risk.

conclusion: Every effort should be made to love and *protect* this unique individual.

m writes: 'Experts are generally agreed that a child's first four or five years shape the way he feels about the world and himself for the rest of his life. If I'd been around more when you were growing up, maybe things would have turned out differently. As it is, 007, please note that despite what your biographer claimed, you only live *once*. I wish you and I had known each other better, but there it is. No use crying over spilt milk. Anyway, promise me you'll get to know your own son. You may think you have all the time in the world. You haven't. No one has.
Are you, are you,
M.'

* * *

Using my black oxidised Ronson lighter, I set fire to M's secret communication. When it was ablaze, I dropped the document out of the window and watched it turn to ash in the gutter. Then I locked the car and re-entered the hospital.

When the lift doors opened on the fifth floor, I was astonished to see Tracy standing there with James in her arms. They were both crying. My first thought was that Shatterheart had shown his true colours and that Tracy and the baby were being pursued by a host of black-clad henchmen armed with machine guns. I stepped out of the lift and looked to left and right. We were quite alone. Tracy leaned against me and sobbed. A piercing, heartrending sob that made my scalp crawl.

'I'm sorry,' she gasped.

'What for? Tracy, what is it?'

Her face was pink, contorted by misery. Her nose was dripping. She looked like a frightened little girl. 'Your dad's dead.'

'What?'

She sniffed and shook her head. 'M's dead, John. He died in his sleep.'

10

Love And Let Die

I don't know why it came as such a surprise. My father was old and ill, and a patient in an NHS hospital. None of these factors had augured well for his recovery. But dead? Before I had even begun to know him, or done one per cent of the things that I had always planned to do with him when he was an old doting father and I was a rich and successful son? It was unbelievable.

My dad, who always voted Labour and cared about the workers despite his close involvement with MI6, had ceased to exist. He could no longer grunt when I asked him a question that required a detailed reply, or blindly defend the police when they were once again found guilty of corruption on a staggering scale, or refer to politicians he secretly hated as 'very clever people'.

During visits home, I would never again hear Dad in the bathroom, making that weird hooting sea-lion noise that he emitted when he swilled water over his newly shaved face. Followed by the long ecologically unsound *Hiss* of the

Cossack hairspray canister as he glued his thin iron-grey curls to his skull.

Nor would I draw back the bedroom curtains to see him sidling slyly into the garage, his cupped right hand trailing a thin spiral of smoke from a cigarette that he could not possibly be smoking, oh no. Because as we all know, M renounced cigarettes after his triple heart bypass and was far too sensible to undo his surgeon's hard work with any further indulgence in this filthiest of habits.

Never again would he ask: 'Are you all right for money?' with that sad, worried look in his eyes, pretend to accept my cheery assurances, then wait until the last possible instant at the railway station to cram two crumpled twenty-pound notes into my hand. 'No, Dad, please.' 'Take it. *Take it*. You never know when you might need it . . .'

Stupidly, what upset me most was knowing that I had beaten M at arm wrestling. I challenged him to a contest when I was about twenty-four. My dad must have been about sixty. He accepted the challenge readily, seemingly convinced that he could humiliate me. I won effortlessly. His arm felt as it was stuffed with crêpe paper. M was a bit annoyed. He seemed to think that he couldn't have been beaten by my real arm, that I must have been using Oddjob's arm instead. If only I'd known he was going to die. I might have let him win.

I was revisited by the pity that overwhelmed me at all those seaside shows when I was a boy. M was dead, and he didn't deserve to be. When M heard that someone he knew had died of cancer or suffered some grim misfortune, he always used to say, in his quiet, understated Salford way: 'It's a bit rough.'

It was a bit rough, all right. Both the event and the world in which it had taken place were intolerably rough. And the Divine Being that had hurled my father into this mortal sphere was rough in every sense; wild, ill-mannered, unjust, uncaring, unpleasant, violent, crude; arbitrary and imprecise to the point of bedlam.

My father's life had been extinguished. I could not talk to the old man, touch him, irritate him or be irritated by him ever again. I wouldn't hear him crooning popular melodies in the flat, tone-deaf voice that made my mother say: 'Oh Myles, give over.' He would no longer embarrass me in front of girlfriends by doing an antiquated dance called 'the twist' when he was feeling merry at New Year.

I would not see him tomorrow or the day after that. I would not see him for the rest of my life. Admittedly, after I had left home, I had sometimes gone for months without speaking to him. But I had always known that his low, throaty, even-tempered voice was a mere phonecall away. Now, no red telephone in creation could connect us.

After breaking the news to me, Tracy sat on the battered mattress in Room 4 and said: 'Why do only good people die? Why couldn't my dad die?'

'You don't mean that.'

'Yes I do. He's a fat, selfish bastard who's no use to anyone. But he'll probably live to be ninety, while someone really kind and worthwhile like your dad dies at the age of seventy-one. Where's the logic in that?'

I left her to cry. Tears were Tracy's way of dealing with pain. The luxury of grieving was denied to me. As a double-0 operative, it was my duty to be as cool about death as a surgeon. James stirred in his cot and started to whimper. Calmly, I scooped him up in one arm and laid him on his mother's lap. Then I went out to ring my brother.

I only had to hear Richard's voice to know it was true. He sounded hoarse and tired, much as he had sounded months before when he rang to tell me about Dad's entry into hospital. 'M's gone and had a stroke, the blithering old fool,' he had said then, artfully turning near-fatal apoplexy into a music-hall comedy routine. Today, however, there were to be no jokes.

'Have you seen him?' I asked, suspecting a hoax.

'Yeah,' my brother sighed. 'I got a call from the hospital early this morning. They wanted me to break the news to Mum. So I drove home and got back by about eight. When I told her, she thought I was lying. I didn't believe it either. But I took her to identify him, and then we both *had* to believe it, really.'

'Let me get this straight: you're saying Dad's been dead all day? And you've only just got round to telling me?'

He sighed. 'Yeah, I know. Sorry. But you're under enough stress as it is. I didn't want to make things worse.' (Double the danger! Double the stress! The hotter the danger, the cooler he takes it!)

The staff on the stroke ward had been shocked by my father's abrupt departure. But someone had wanted the old man out of the way, and I had no idea who. All I knew was that it wasn't Shatterheart. He was just a surgeon who didn't know my father, and who had probably never even seen a Bond film.

On the following day, the day before the funeral, I caught the

1400 from Euston to Manchester. I travelled first class. The old man would have wanted it that way.

Tracy adored M. She would have liked to have said her last goodbye to him. But the baby's operation was a mere three days away. It made sense for her to stay at Great Ormond Street with James, while I went back to Stockport to say goodbye on her behalf.

As the train rattled north, I listened to music on my Walkman: John Barry's soundtrack for *The Living Daylights*. I bought a gin-and-tonic from the buffet (the young man behind the bar nervously explained that he wasn't authorised to mix vodka martinis) and sipped it slowly, letting Barry's immaculate orchestrations wash over me.

The Living Daylights may well have signalled the end of John Barry's involvement with the Bond series. Like his score for *OHMSS*, it was intended to launch a new James Bond: this time, Timothy Dalton. The next two films in the series, *Licence To Kill* and *Goldeneye*, were not scored by JB (the finest initials in the world) and believe me, it shows. It's possible that Barry became too expensive for the producers of *Goldeneye*, which by Bond standards was fairly low-budget. Or perhaps John simply couldn't face arranging my justifiably renowned theme tune for the thousandth time.

In my opinion, any sentence that begins with the words 'in my opinion' is highly suspect. Notwithstanding this, in my opinion John Barry is one of the greatest composers of all time, not just of film scores, but of serious music. And by serious, I mean all music that is thrilling and moving, all music that turns our thoughts and emotions to the infinite, whether it's performed by the LSO or by small children banging pots.

(Incidentally, I always hated that moment in *Goldfinger* when Bond says that drinking unchilled Dom Pérignon '53 is like listening to The Beatles without ear-muffs. What rubbish. I always loved The Beatles. *Goldfinger* also has a repulsive moment when Bond gets rid of a woman by slapping her on the arse and saying: 'Man-talk.' I would never dream of being such a slob. How odd that my favourite Bond film contains two scenes that utterly misrepresent me.) I returned to the buffet to buy some Benzedrine, but the young man behind the counter could only offer me crisps and hot bacon and tomato rolls. It wasn't the young man's fault. For him, for all employees of British Rail, life had always been too easy and too soft.

I turned and headed back to my carriage. M's face drifted before my eyes and I felt weak and dizzy. I thought, I can get through this thing. Like 007, 'the hotter the danger, the cooler I take it!' In *You Only Live Twice*, Sir James Molony, nerve specialist by appointment to the Service, observed that James Bond's spirit was strong enough to survive ordeals that would break any normal man. The same thing was obviously true of me. I would undoubtedly survive my father's death, and whatever lay beyond.

Then my knees buckled. Someone caught me, heaved me upright and helped me to my seat. 'Hey now, take it easy . . .'

I shook my head to ease the dizziness and found myself looking, in amazement, at a sad hawk-like face that I knew and loved. 'Felix Leiter!' I exclaimed. 'What the hell are you doing here?'

'Came to pay my respects,' drawled the straw-haired Texan. 'I heard about your daddy.'

I scowled ruefully. 'Can't keep any secrets from the CIA . . .'

Leiter slit open a pack of King Size Chesterfields with his one good hand. 'If you'd studied your Ian Fleming, you'd know I haven't worked for the CIA in a long while. I joined Pinkertons in *Diamonds Are Forever*. What's wrong, 007? You losing your touch?'

My eyes became fierce slits. 'Far from it. In fact, I happen to know that the CIA called you out of retirement to help with the *Thunderball* affair. So who's losing their touch now?'

'Pardon me for breathing.'

'No, Felix. It's me who should apologise. I'm just a bit under the weather. I thought the old man and me had all the time in the world. One thing I'm learning is that there's never enough time.'

Leiter lit two Chesterfields with a Zippo lighter and passed one to me. We drew the fragrant, carcinogenic smoke deep into our lungs. Then Leiter said: 'James, nothing is forever. You know that. Even diamonds have had it if you drop them in a glass of Coke. You've loved many women and killed Christ knows how many crooks in your time. God doesn't protect the beasts of the field and the li'l ol' sparrows. He lets 'em rot. You know that. Same with your chief, there. Your entire family have got lousy arteries. It's a congenital defect. And when you clog up those goddamned tubes with bacon fat and cigarette smoke, what the hell do you expect?'

My eyes became fierce slits again. 'Go to hell, Felix. Or

read Chapter 21 of *You Only Live Twice*, where it clearly states that I'm not about to waste my days by trying to prolong them. Or consider that beautifully directed casino scene in *Goldeneye*, where I state that my recipe for living is "Enjoy it while it lasts."'

Leiter grinned ironically. 'If only that were true.'

'Shut up. It is true.'

'OK. OK. Don't get sore. All I'm saying is, when M sent you to that health farm in *Thunderball*, he knew what he was doing. You're chock-a-block full of toxins, 007. But you still pour salt all over your goddamned scrambled eggs, just like he did.

'It's plumb crazy. If I lose the use of my right arm, it makes no damn' difference. My right arm was bitten off by a shark in *Live And Let Die*. But if *you* lose your gun-hand, you can kiss goodbye to that licence to kill. Think it over, Bond.'

I pointed to the cigarette burning in the corner of his mouth. 'I will if you will.'

Decisively, Leiter snatched the Chesterfield out of his mouth and stamped on it. Then he took the almost-full carton out of his jacket and squashed it flat with the heel of his boot. 'OK. Now it's your turn,' he challenged.

I shook my head and blew smoke in his face. 'You're forgetting something. The way my life is at the moment, smoking and drinking are the only things that keep me from going under.'

'Big deal,' said Leiter petulantly. 'You think you're the only one who gets depressed?'

I studied the tall Texan seriously. 'What have you got to be depressed about?'

'Never having a real purpose,' admitted Leiter resignedly.

'You had a purpose,' I reminded him staunchly. 'You were always my best friend in America . . .'

'Thanks, pal. But you know as well as I do that I was only in the Bond books because Fleming wanted to conquer the American market. Trouble was, I bored Americans as much as I bored everyone else. I never did anything interesting because you were the hero. I was superfluous to the plots. Fleming knew it, his readers knew it and I guess you knew it too . . .'

I shrugged apologetically. 'Sorry you feel that way.'

'Wasn't just the books,' insisted Leiter. 'I was miscast in all the goddamned films. None of those actors looked a goddamned thing like me, apart from Rik Van Nutter in *Thunderball*, and who the hell wants to be played by a Nutter?'

'Good point.' The smile that had briefly lit my blue-grey eyes quickly faded. 'But you've come a long way, Felix. Is this all you've got to tell me?'

Leiter studied me affectionately. 'Nope. Guess there is a bit more.'

'Go ahead.'

'You've been ill, John. I guess what's been happening with your wife and baby has screwed you up pretty bad. But I've been on this case as long as you have. I've had me some time to think. Maybe your son really *does* have a hole in the heart.'

I nodded and smiled. 'You'll be telling me I'm not James Bond, next.'

Leiter gave me a sideways glance and sighed. 'You've been under a helluva lotta pressure, what with your old man dying and your kid getting sick and all.' He gazed at the green fields speeding past the window, then fixed me with his candid gaze. 'But you've gotta stop running away. Maybe it's time to admit to the pain, ol' buddy.'

'What pain? I haven't got much heart. None of us double-0 operatives have.'

'Then why did you have a breakdown when your wife was killed in *OHMSS*?'

'Don't be so bloody personal.'

'James, we're all damaged goods – every last one of us. Quit carrying it all around with you. Feel the pain, forgive and move on.'

'Felix, I haven't the damnedest idea what you're talking about.'

The straw-haired Texan grinned. 'You'll figure it out.' Leiter got off the train at Stoke-on-Trent, despite my assurances that Stoke was no match for Royale-les-Eaux. As the train pulled away from the station, Leiter grinned his boyish grin and raised his steel hook in farewell. A lump came to my throat as I watched him limp along the platform. Whenever my missions had taken me to America, Felix Leiter had shown me nothing but kindness. He had never pointed out that the CIA despise the British Secret Service, or reminded me that a British agent, licensed to kill or not, would have had no jurisdiction on American soil. For this, I would always be grateful to him.

Richard met me on the platform at Stockport station. He looked pale and sad. His eyes were ringed by dark shadows, and he had a painful-looking pimple on the side of his nose. The sight of my brother and his pimple filled me with love, and I embraced him. Normally, Richard shrinks from physical contact. Today he hugged me back. This was a special occasion. It isn't every week that your father dies.

After the obligatory three seconds (any all-male embrace that lasts longer may be construed as evidence of homosexuality) I felt Richard stiffen self-consciously, straining to free himself. Reluctantly, I let go.

Then my mother stepped out of the shadows.

She was draped in my dad's sheepskin jacket, which was about five sizes too big for her. I glanced down to see if she was wearing the shiny buttoned boots with the deadly toe caps. But no, she was wearing a pair of sensible old-lady shoes that looked as if they came from Clarkes.

Mum's face didn't look combative any more. Only tired and inexpressibly forlorn. Not that this impressed me. I found it perfectly credible that she had loved M, while secretly working for the other side. In the first Bond novel, *Casino Royale*, Vesper Lynd demonstrated the same emotional confusion. Vesper was unable to choose between me and SMERSH, so killed herself. There's a lot of it about.

Then my mother grasped me briefly and said: 'Hello love. Are you all right?' (What did she mean by that? What was she trying to imply?)

We walked out to the car park. Mum and Richard wanted to know about Tracy and the baby, so I gave them a succinct up-date. Richard had hired a car, a snug little Peugeot. Mum sat in the front with Richard and I slumped in the back, and we drove out onto Wellington Road, where throughout my teens

I'd queued for the bus after countless depressing nights at the now-extinct Classic Cinema.

Stockport College passed by on my right. I'd taken an arts foundation course at Stockport College in the late seventies. I didn't really want to be a painter, or an advertising copy-writer, or any of the things I've been. All I ever wanted to do was stay in luxurious hotels, drive exquisite cars, make love to beautiful women without the risk of emotional involvement and kill any bastard who stood in my way.

Richard had a cold, and Mum wanted some stamps so we drove into Poynton where there was a chemist and a Post Office. On the way, my mother glanced at me, smiled and said: 'Angliski Spion.' A chill of horror passed through me. This was what Rosa Klebb called Bond in *From Russia With Love*. Good God. And in front of my brother, too. The bitch was being damned cool about it. Or had Richard been working for Redland all along?

She went on to say: 'Me and your dad used to love walking there on a Sunday afternoon.'

I relaxed, realising that I'd misheard her. She'd said 'Anglesey Drive', not 'Angliski Spion'. Just as Richmond Road is the best road in all Jamaica (*Dr No*, Chapter one, paragraph three) so is Anglesey Drive the finest road in walking distance of my parents' house. Mum and Dad liked to walk up and down Anglesey Drive, speculating about which house they would buy if they inherited enough money. Although I don't know who they thought was likely to leave them this hypothetical fortune. Most of their relations were even poorer than they were.

'Any chance of seeing Dad before the funeral?' I asked,

getting the emphasis all wrong so that it sounded as if I was asking if M fancied going out for a pint before he was cremated.

Mum shifted awkwardly in her seat. Richard, adopting his loudest, clearest, 'sensible-son' voice said: 'Er, I rang the undertaker to ask about that. He said that he, er, wouldn't advise it.'

This chilled me. Because M's death had been unexpected, there had been a full autopsy. What had they done to him? Sliced off the top of his head, then replaced it back to front, so that it looked as if he was wearing an ill-fitting beret? I wouldn't have put it past the bastards!

Later, when we entered our parents' house, the stillness and the silence were absolute. My mouth went dry as I looked at the empty armchair where my father used to slump after a hard day's work. Then another line out of *From Russia With Love* sprang to mind. 'This wonderful man who carried the sun with him'.

In Fleming's novel, this was a description of Darko Kerim, my contact in Istanbul, whose life was cut cruelly short aboard the Orient Express. But it was equally applicable to my father, who could light up a room with his warmth and good humour. Especially on Saturday nights, when he came home pissed.

While Mum busied herself in the kitchen, making tea, Richard told me about seeing M dead at the hospital. 'I know it's a cliché, but he just looked asleep, just like the times when he used to crash out on the sofa after the wrestling on Saturday afternoon.'

I said, 'You mean the times when he used to take his

shoes off and the smell of his socks would stink up the whole house.'

I began to laugh. This wonderful man who carried the sun with him, and only had a bath once a week. Richard started laughing too, and then abruptly, in mid-guffaw, his face crumpled and he began to weep silently. It was like something in a film – but not a Bond film. The shock of the emotion Richard was experiencing made him gasp. His breathing became sharp and rapid as if he'd stepped under an ice-cold shower.

'Oh, Rich,' I said, and took hold of his arm. Immediately, I felt him resist, so I took my hand away. Mum came in with a tea tray and a plate heaped with a fine selection of stale biscuits. While we were drinking our tea, a nice young curate called Robin arrived to find out something about M. Robin was handling tomorrow's funeral service. Because Robin didn't know my father from Ernst Stavro Blofeld, he was obliged to ask us for any interesting titbits or facts we could provide about the deceased.

'In many ways Myles was an ordinary chap with ordinary interests,' my mother volunteered unhelpfully.

'That's true,' I wanted to add. 'When my girlfriends used to sunbathe in the garden, I remember Dad sneaking sly glances at their tits.'

Pleasant as Robin was, I couldn't tell him the most important fact of all: that M had been the Head of the British Secret Service. So I remained cold and watchful, probably making the same impression on Robin that I made on the murderous Major Smythe in the short story of *Octopussy*: dark, dangerous and although not unpleasant, definitely not a man to meddle with.

Robin was about thirty: tall, lean and handsome, with an exquisitely gentle face. You could tell that he was the rare kind of Christian who was more interested in loving people than locking them out of the Kingdom of Heaven. M, who admired human decency above all things, would have instantly warmed to Robin and called him a 'smashing lad'. But M was dead.

So when Robin offered to read an excerpt from a book of our choice, I didn't bother to suggest the opening page of *Goldfinger*, as appropriate as it would have been. Nor, when he asked which record we wished to hear as we filed out at the end of the service, did I mention Tom Jones's rousing version of *Thunderball*, the theme song to the first film I ever went to see with my father.

Because this funeral, this bland farce that was intended to signal the end of M's life, had been arranged by my mother and by Richard, her favourite son. It had nothing to do with me or the M I knew, the man who masterminded British Intelligence from the cramped little office of an impoverished printing firm. The man who loved me in secret. So I left Mum and Richard to it and went upstairs, just as I'd done as a child. I lay on the bed in my room and tried to cry.

But still the tears wouldn't come. Of course they wouldn't. As René Mathis pointed out in *Casino Royale*, I am more of a machine than a human being. A killing machine. My father's death was regrettable, but hardly unexpected. To hell with sentiment! M smoked and drank and worked himself into the ground for his family. The selfish old bastard! To cap it all, he'd deserted me at the worst time of my life.

Christ, I loved him.

To cheer myself up, I stared up at the ceiling and thought of my favourite moments from the Bond films – the moments when M laughed.

Because of my unfeasibly retentive memory, I can remember exactly where M laughed in every Bond film that we watched together. In *Thunderball*, he laughed three times during the pre-credits sequence; once when I punched the man dressed as a woman, again when I flew away from my enemies by using a jet-pack and lastly when my Aston Martin repelled my pursuing enemies with a high-pressure water jet.

M beamed in admiration during Maurice Binder's title sequence. Perhaps he was smiling at John Barry's *Thunderball* theme tune, not one of John's best but still better than anything any other fucker could have written. Then again, M's pleasure might have been inspired by the silhouetted nipples of the female swimmers.

After the credits, M laughed a total of twenty-nine times. When he wasn't laughing, he was smiling. Despite its lethargic underwater sequences, *Thunderball* is a very witty film.

Dr No elicited five laughs from my father, as did *From Russia With Love*. In both these films, humour was the icing on the cake, rather than the actual cake mix. But in *Diamonds Are Forever*, where everything was played for laughs, M didn't laugh once. Nor can I blame Roger Moore – much as I'd like to. Because in *Diamonds*, Bond was portrayed by Sean, who had recovered from his for-God's-sake-I'm-bored appearance in *You Only Live*

Twice to play Bond as he had never been played before: cynical, classless, icily cold. But apart from a gritty fight in a lift (always cut for television) and a slick car chase through the streets of Las Vegas, the film of *Diamonds Are Forever* is tedious. But nowhere near as tedious as the novel.

A word about Roger Moore. My dad laughed twice during *Live And Let Die*; once when Bond escaped the hungry crocodiles by using them as stepping stones, and again during the climax of the speedboat chase when Bond throws petrol into the eyes of Adam, Mr Big's henchman, causing his boat to collide with a navy landing ship. In the course of *The Spy Who Loved Me*, which we watched on TV together one bank holiday afternoon, M laughed seven times.

Unlike me, M was scrupulously fair. He had nothing against Roger Moore. M simply preferred the Bond films when they were thrillers laced by wit, as opposed to the unfunny comedies with a few farcical thrills attached that they became in the 1970s. *Moonraker* is a woefully long way from *Goldfinger*.

M claimed that he'd seen *Goldfinger* at the cinema on its original release in 1964. I don't know whether this was true or not. Unlike me, Dad had an appalling memory. When *Thunderball* was shown on TV for the first time, M and I watched it again together. He laughed in all the right places – twenty-nine in all – and when it was over had the temerity to say: 'That wasn't bad. I haven't seen that one before.'

So perhaps M really did see *Goldfinger* without me. Perhaps he led an entire life that I have no knowledge of. I am willing to entertain this possibility for the following reason: Maurice, a friend of my father's, Maurice whom I trust, once told me that he'd heard my father say 'fuck'. 'Really?' I marvelled. 'You've really heard him "f and blind"?' 'Not often,' said Maurice. 'But I have heard him.'

This awakened me to a whole universe of bizarre possibilities. If my father could swear, he could also get erections. If he could sustain those erections, he could have sexual intercourse. If he had sex, then he might be fertile. If he was fertile, I might be his son. If I was his son, he might have loved me.

He never said so, but nor did he tell me that he had sex. He definitely never said 'fuck' in front of me, although I saw him thinking it once or twice, usually when I walked out of a job for the umpteenth time.

Once, I actually had a conversation with my father. Picture the cheap Day-glo sign outside the Davenport Cinema, a sign so cheap-looking that only my dad could have painted it. The sign reads: 'Now showing, for one night only, your father as you'd like to remember him.'

It happened in the early eighties. My first girlfriend had just dumped me. For a man who viewed women as 'recreation', I was taking it rather badly. I came home and disgraced myself by breaking down in front of my parents.

M leapt up and turned off the TV. That was the rule in our house. Whenever something important was happening, Dad turned off the telly. 'Son, son. What's the matter?'

I wailed, unable to control myself. Despite being 'the envy of every man, the idol of every woman', my life had fallen apart.

To my amazement, M took me out for a drink. I'd never been out for a drink with Dad before, not just me and him.

We'd been to the pictures together, to see Bond films, but never the pub. I don't know why. This night, over a few soothing pints, I asked Dad all the things I'd never bothered to ask him. Kindly, indulgently, he answered me.

'Do you agree that the Tories should be shot, Dad?'

'No, son. I don't agree with any kind of killing.'

'What about racism?'

'No. I've seen what racism can do. We should fight it in others and in ourselves.'

'What about that time, years ago, when you hit me at that cricket match?'

'What cricket match?'

'On holiday. You fell asleep at a cricket match. You were getting sunstroke so I tried to wake you.'

'And I clouted you, did I?'

'Yeah. Don't you remember?'

He shook his head and laughed. 'You're not still mad at me after all this time, are you?'

'No. I just don't know why you did it.'

'Maybe I *wanted* to get sunstroke.'

'Do you agree with hitting children?'

He considered this for a few moments. 'No.' He smiled. 'I don't agree with it. I've done it, but I don't agree with it.'

'Hey! What else don't you agree with, Dad?'

'I don't agree that you should waste your time worrying about young girls who don't know any better. I don't agree that you should fail your exams because of them.'

'Dad, I'll probably fail my exams anyway.'

'I agree.'

I wondered who he was, this warm, wise man that I'd been living with for all those years. We'd eaten at the same table, been on holiday together, slept in adjacent rooms. How come I'd never noticed him before? To quote from *Goldfinger*, the level of my ignorance was 'Shocking. Positively shocking.'

Goldfinger, although not flawless, is still a cinematic jewel. In *Goldfinger*, the best James Bond gives his best performance as 007 and the screenwriters deliver their slickest, most impudent script. Gert Frobe as Goldfinger and Harold Sakata as Oddjob are beyond the shadow of an industrial laser the most menacing villains in the series. Add Guy Hamilton's brisk direction, Peter Hunt's masterful editing and John Barry's impeccable score and you have the recipe for the finest Bond film ever.

Which brings me to a sad confession. I never had the pleasure of watching *Goldfinger* with my father. Last Christmas, when Tracy and I spent the holidays in Hazel Grove, I deliberately engineered a *Goldfinger*-watching situation by asking Mum and Dad to buy me a digitally remastered video of the third James Bond film. What could be more natural than watching a Christmas present from my parents in their presence?

On Christmas morning, everything went according to plan. While Dad and I were sharing our first beer of the day, I slipped *Goldfinger* into the VCR and let it play. Dad and Tracy were chatting together on the sofa. My mother was in the kitchen, fretting about the turkey. As the pre-credits sequence rolled, M started to show interest. He laughed three times, as I'd correctly predicted.

Dad's first laugh. I peel off my frogman suit to reveal an immaculate white tuxedo.

Dad's second laugh. I justify my habit of carrying a firearm with the words: 'I have a slight inferiority complex.'

Dad's last laugh. I electrocute the Mexican bandit and quip: 'Shocking. Positively shocking.'

But after the titles, when I slapped Dink's arse and sent her packing, M cringed in embarrassment. 'Isn't it awful?' he laughed, red-faced and ashamed that his beloved daughter-in-law should have witnessed such a misogynistic moment of cinema. Still blushing, M led Tracy out to his greenhouse to show her his tomatoes. He didn't actually have any tomatoes. That was how embarrassed he was.

Admitting defeat, I ejected *Goldfinger* from the machine and replaced it in its case. I sympathised with M. As I've said before, I'm not in the habit of smacking women's bottoms. That scene with Dink never happened. It was fabricated by the screenwriters. I may have slapped a few women across the face in my time: notably in the films *From Russia With Love*, *Diamonds Are Forever* and *The Man With The Golden Gun*. But each of these slaps was strictly in the line of duty.

But if M had given *Goldfinger* a chance, I'm fairly certain that he would have laughed a total of twenty-two times. Sadly, it was not to be.

And why this singular obession with my father laughing? Because as he laughed, he would always glance down at me to see if I was laughing too. I invariably was, whether I got the joke or not, because those moments of shared warmth with my father meant more to me than all the Bond books and films put together.

* * *

The next morning, I awoke early. Before visiting the bathroom for my customary ice-cold shower, I lay on my back and stared at the bedroom door. In the mornings, throughout my early life, this door was usually opened by Mum, coming in to wake me for school or college or to remind me to sign on.

M's face popped round the door less often, usually to tell me good things or extremely sad things. On the penultimate Saturday in August, when we were bound for the seaside, Dad's face would always appear minus its dentures. He'd wake me by whistling tunelessly, then saying 'Hols', pronouncing this word: 'Holth' because of his missing teeth.

The same face, considerably less happy, would sometimes appear to say: 'You shouldn't hit your mother.' Once I had the ill grace to say: 'But she hit me first.' Then pain in his eyes as he said: 'I don't care. You should never hit a woman.' ('But Dad: she's not just any woman. She's the Head of Operations for SMERSH . . .')

Years later, during the summer holidays, Dad would poke his face into my room at a grotesquely early hour to rouse me for some dirty, gruelling factory job. He'd always be dressed, his collar crisp and his stripy tie straight, the aroma of Cossack hairspray emanating from his greying maritime head. On these mornings, M would be neither happy or sad, merely business-like: his business being to ensure that his shiftless student son worked for at least two weeks out of every year.

'OK!' he'd bark briskly, false teeth firmly in place. 'Time for work.'

M thought that work was important, no matter how menial or poorly paid the job. In the evenings, after work, I sometimes told him how lazy the men that I worked with were, how they spent their days farting, swearing and picking horses. I told him how I had found four grown men hiding behind a crate, playing poker when they were meant to be building diesel engines. One of the card players looked up, saw me and said: 'Fuck off, you lazy student.'

When I told this story to M, he didn't laugh. 'It's stealing,' he fumed. 'I'd do anything, I'd sweep the streets, anything but be idle like that.' I knew that M was telling the truth. Dad was a workaholic. Why else would he have chosen to hold down two jobs, juggling a demanding role as Head of the Secret Service with his troubled, poorly paid printing career?

One summer morning, when M came in to rouse me for my holiday job, I told him that I was too hungover to go to work. M called me a 'bone-idle sod'. He spat the insult with real venom. Had he been a bully – he was never that – he would have tried to drag me out of bed. Instead, he went away to calm down and returned three minutes later with an apology and the offer of a lift to work. It was an offer that no reasonable son could have refused.

M's faith in the Victorian work ethic was dealt a death blow on the day he was fired by the firm he'd devoted his life to. That night, when he came home from work, M tripped over my shoes which I'd lazily abandoned in the middle of the hallway. Although unhurt, he flew at me in a wild fury. I had never seen him so angry, or known him to react so heatedly to such a minor misdemeanour.

As M swore at me and threatened me, his fists were clenched and he was shaking. My dad was simply dying to hit me. But

I was young and fit. M knew, beyond all possible doubt that, had he taken a swipe at me, I would have knocked him to the ground. That, I am sure, is the only reason he stayed his hand: a fact which shames us both.

In the morning, while M was at work, Mum tearfully explained his uncharacteristic behaviour. The managing director hadn't even had the decency to sack M in private. He'd assembled the work-force and in front of them, told my dad his services were no longer required.

That evening, while I was reading in my room, the door opened and Dad's face appeared. He was smiling, his old self again. 'Listen,' he said. 'I'm sorry for flaring up at you.' 'That's OK,' I said. I was twenty-one, but he walked into the room and ruffled my hair as if I was ten years old. 'I want us to be mates,' he said. 'Are we mates?'

If this scene had occurred in a Hollywood film, I would then have thrown my arms around M and sobbed: 'I love you, Dad.' And he would have hugged me back, his voice choking with emotion as he answered: 'I love you too, son.'

But we lived in Hazel Grove, a village near the town of Stockport in north-west England. We were Englishmen, taught to hide our emotions from birth. Neither of us would have been comfortable with a big show of sentiment. So I gripped my dad's hand in a suitably manly fashion and said: 'I don't know. What do you reckon, Dad?'

Gratified, he nodded and laughed. 'Oh, I think we can just about tolerate each other.'

M's funeral had the dark familiarity of a dimly recalled

nightmare. The church was full of M's friends, neighbours, relations and old work-mates. I sat at the front of the church with my brother and my mother, unable to take the proceedings seriously. By rights, as a retired Admiral in the British Navy, Dad should have been buried at sea.

Mum and Richard had chosen the hymns, including 'Amazing Grace'. As a tribute to my father, I dispensed with this song's morbid lyrics and sang: 'Are you, are you' all the way through. Then Robin told everyone about Myles Bryce, a man he'd never met, but who was apparently well liked and had a number of keen interests including gardening, cricket and motoring. Robin seemed to be saying that although Dad wasn't a Christian, his reassuringly commonplace hobbies would guarantee him a place on God's right hand.

Robin also described Dad as a man who felt a lot but, like many men of his generation, was too reserved to give voice to his feelings. This wasn't strictly true. The last time that I saw M, he made his feelings plain to all of us.

We were at the hospital. It was the time of our evening visit. Yesterday, M had blown raspberries at Mum. Tonight, his mood was considerably more sanguine. M, Tracy, Mum and I were sitting around a small table in a dimly lit, cheaply furnished corridor that was laughably referred to as 'the day room'. It would have been more honest to call it the 'overpowering smell of urine' room or 'the TV is insanely loud' room.

M's right ankle was already badly swollen by the clot that would shortly kill him. Physiotherapy might have prevented this clot from forming. An intelligent doctor might have identified the tell-tale swelling. But the NHS was in its death throes. Physiotherapists and doctors, intelligent or otherwise, were in short supply. M hadn't even been given anything to support his leg. Tracy had to scour the hospital to find him a footstool.

M's complexion was a worrying shade of brownish-yellow, as if he was already trying on his death-mask for size. There was a bad smell coming off him that I couldn't place at all. But his spirits were high. He wouldn't stop singing.

He sang 'Baa Baa Black Sheep' to the baby in his lap. Or 'Are you, are you', as it is sometimes known. To his wife he sang an 'Are You' remix of 'O Mio Bambino Caro'.

Despite the ghastly circumstances, it was a very happy hour. When he wasn't singing, M was playfully flicking elastic bands at Tracy. He had not been so animated or cheerful since his stroke. We all believed that we were finally witnessing the first signs of his recovery.

When it was time to leave, M didn't cry or exhibit the slightest trace of unhappiness. Instead, he placed his good hand on James's head and said, with quiet warmth: 'Are you.'

Then he leaned over to touch Tracy and my mother on the head in the same way, repeating the same benediction. 'Are you . . . are you.' Lastly he touched my head, winking at me as he did so. 'Are you,' said M. 'You, you.'

The church was filled to capacity. A group of Dad's former apprentices stood at the back. During the service, I heard one of them sobbing. I half-expected M to sit up in his coffin, then nod to Richard and me: 'That's young Colin from work you can hear crying. He's a smashing little mourner.'

Or for the casket itself, customised by those clever chaps at Q Branch, to sprout wings and jet down the aisle.

Robin read a piece of prose that had been chosen by Richard; something about how the dead haven't died, they've simply gone into the next room. If this was true, why were they never in the next room when you walked into it?

The answer was simple. Because this was the real world, the same ugly, crushingly dull world that I used to blink at in dazed disbelief whenever I left the cinema after a Bond film. The coffin on the stage was destined for a furnace. John Barry had not composed an eerie elegy to accompany its passage into the flames. Unlike Sean in *Diamonds Are Forever*, my dad was not about to escape cremation because of some confusing plot twist that no one in the audience could follow.

I wondered if M ever thought what I was thinking as he drove me home from the Davenport Cinema in some crap second-hand car which he was buying on hire-purchase. Was he thinking: 'Where's my vodka martini, shaken not stirred? Why am I smoking Players? Where are the specially blended cigarettes with the three gold bands made for me by Morland of St Jermyn Street, with a gun-metal cigarette case to keep them in? Where are my three exciting missions a year? Not to mention my two months' leave? Where are my new incredible women? I only seem to attract incredibly old women. As for that bugger who overtook me at the traffic lights, where's my heat-seeking missile? I want to blow him up. What about my Chelsea flat, my adorable secretary, my snorkel, my suntan, my attaché case, my health farm, my tailor, my enormous shoulders? What about my Scottish accent? My witty one-liners?

A Sean Connery toupee wouldn't come amiss. Where's my hotel suite, my seat at the casino, my beach, my sky, my ocean? *Where is my life?*'

When people walk away from a funeral, they do so hesitantly, walking in slow motion lest anyone should think them indecently eager to escape the scene of death. My mother, brother and I left first in order to stand in the vestibule, greeting the hesitant mourners as they filed by. People I knew well or vaguely recognised or had never seen before in my life shuffled past and shook our hands.

I saw myself reflected in their eyes, rather as Bond saw his would-be assassin in the eyes of Bonita the flamenco dancer in the opening teaser sequence for *Goldfinger*. I saw people flinch inperceptibly as they took in my gaunt, ill face. I know that my dad, as ill as he was, as ebullient as I pretended to be, must have seen a similar look of hurt and surprise in my face when I first saw him after his stroke. Perhaps that was why he held my hand for a full minute.

Some of the mourners made kind remarks, others mumbled apologetically, most simply said that they were sorry. The only poorly judged comment came from my Aunt Dot, who said: 'Nice funeral. Your dad would have liked it.'

During the service, my mother had remained dry-eyed and composed. But as she was leaving the church, she swooned. My brother caught her as she fell. Robin joined forces with Richard to lift her into the back of the funeral car. The undertakers were rather put out by this sudden break with protocol, and sulked all the way to the crematorium.

* * *

Afterwards, a number of friends and relatives came to the house for drinks and sandwiches. Throughout the proceedings, my mum sat on the sofa, clutching a glass of whisky in a shaking hand. When the guests had left, taking their awkward small-talk with them, a few female neighbours tidied up and cleared away the dishes.

And then there was just my brother and I, alone with my mother in the house we were born in. Richard was staying the night. But I had to get back to Great Ormond Street. Now, I had a new mission. The hardest but potentially the most rewarding mission of my Intelligence career. My boy needed a father. Tracy needed a husband. *I* was the only man for the job.

Richard drove me to Stockport station. Mum insisted on accompanying us. I felt sorry for her, deeply sorry. The night before, I'd woken up at about three, bursting for a pee. On the way back from the bathroom, I passed her room and heard her sobbing her heart out, alone in the bedroom that for forty years she had shared with that remarkable man who was the Head of the Secret Service.

I now understood what Felix Leiter had meant when he advised me to admit to the pain and move on. Whatever she thought of me, Mum had worshipped Myles Bryce. Now, like me, she would always miss him. Finally, she and I had something in common.

Was it conceivable that we could now break our neurotic, futile cycle of love and hate and develop a workable relationship? God Almighty, it had to be worth a try.

When it was time for me to board the train, Richard suddenly leaned forward to give me a bashful hug. This surprised me, but then my mother surprised me more. She threw her arms around me, squeezing me hard and wishing me and Tracy and James all the luck in the world. Without a hint of irony in her eyes or voice she said: 'I'll be thinking of you.'

I smiled at her. 'I'll be thinking of you, too.'

Mum stepped back and took my hand in hers. I looked into her face. Her eyes glowed with affection.

As I glanced down at her feet, I saw an inch of thin knife blade emerge from the toe of her navy court shoe. Then my mother kicked me in the shin; a vicious, surprisingly robust kick that made me whistle through my teeth.

'Farewell, Mr Bond,' she whispered.

11

You Only Live Miserably

The scent and sweat of a children's hospital are nauseating at four in the morning. Then the soul-erosion produced by the endless waiting – a compost of anger and pain and sheer bloody terror – becomes unbearable and the senses awake and revolt from it.

Before I opened my eyes, I knew that Tracy was not beside me. Nor was she anywhere in the room. I stood and walked over to the cot where James was sleeping. Lying there, with his ebony-black hair and eyelashes, pale skin made luminous by the dimmed hospital lights, he looked as precious and fragile as a little china doll. Neither his appearance nor his noiseless breathing betrayed the merest trace of the condition that threatened to end his life.

James was wearing a brand-new Winnie the Pooh baby-grow. Tracy and I had gone shopping yesterday, on the eve of his operation. She'd insisted on buying him as many toys and clothes as we could carry. When, after spending over seventy pounds in Hamleys, I carelessly implied that my wife might have been overdoing things, she wept a little and said: 'It's true, I know. But if I don't buy him the things I want to buy him, it's like saying I'm wasting money on someone who isn't going to live. Don't you understand?'

Yes, I understand.

As I stroked the baby's hair, I heard an erratic Er! Er! on the other side of the partition wall to my left. It sounded like a mild-mannered frog with no sense of rhythm. It was actually Edward, a baby in the neighbouring cubicle.

Edward was born with so many things wrong with him that his parents were embarrassed to visit him. He had heart problems, digestive problems and some kind of brain disorder. If that sounds vague, then it's because the nurse I overheard discussing his case was equally vague.

Edward was diminutive because he couldn't feed properly, the only sound he made was Er! Er! and his eyes, which were probably sightless, looked like fried eggs with tiny black yolks. He resembled a badly drawn cartoon. Yet Edward was one of the most loveable children you could ever hope to see.

Edward's father secretly thought so too. He, the baby's mother, and a few noisy relatives, visited Edward for one hour each night. Edward's mother was maniacally cheerful but never picked her baby up. Tracy, who was mad about Edward, thought that his mother was ashamed of giving birth to something so imperfect and that his father, who always picked him up, loved his son *because* he was imperfect.

It certainly looked that way. Mr Edward Senior was a big man with wide shoulders and a broken nose. He could have given Oddjob or Red Grant a run for their money. He held that baby as if he would kill anyone who even suggested anything was wrong with him. Edward was due for a heart operation on the same morning as James. Shatterheart was to be his surgeon.

The little girl in the cubicle to my right started to cry. She was eleven years old, and in desperate need of a heart transplant. Her mother, who accompanied her twenty-four hours a day, started to speak to her in a quiet, calm voice but the girl didn't stop crying. Like Edward, like any child in the hospital, she deserved pity, but I had no pity left. Today, all my prayers, my energy and my compassion were reserved for my son and his journey into a darkness from which he might never return.

Yet in a way, I knew that my emotions were wasted on James. Unlike the crying girl, my son was unaware of his condition. He knew nothing of the gleaming scalpel that would cut open his chest in six hours time. He slept on peacefully while his parents, sick with fear, sweated through the night. Ninety per cent, they'd told us. Out of every ten children operated on, one would die. These odds were not encouraging; particularly when one knew that out of every hundred children, only one is born with any kind of heart defect. So Tracy, the baby and I weren't exactly enjoying a winning streak. If James's heart didn't fail during surgery, it might fail later. The first eight hours after the operation were to be critical.

I slipped into a T-shirt and jeans and walked down the corridor to the men's room. While I was washing my hands, I gazed into the mirror and sighed. There was no trace of irony in my blue-grey eyes. My dark, un-English face didn't look cruel or piratical. Merely anxious, tired and sad.

It had been fun driving halfway across France. But during my trip, I'd come close to a complete mental breakdown. But now Bond was back, ready to face a test that 'needed so much more toughness than he had ever had to show'.

Except I wasn't James Bond, only John Bryce of Hazel Grove near Stockport. I knew that now, while understanding perfectly where my adolescent delusions had come from. For James Bond is the ultimate male fantasy; licensed to kill and to be promiscuous, guaranteed to take control of any difficult situation. 007's essence is power and potency. But nothing is more guaranteed to make a man feel powerless and impotent than placing the life of his only child in the hands of strangers: especially when those strangers seem at worst uncaring and, at best, only moderately competent.

Like my father before me, I had suppressed my feelings for so long that any expression of concern for my son had emerged as slow, sustained anger. A good cry might have helped, but I didn't know how to cry. Instead, I chose to make a virtue of my condition by deliberately identifying with James Bond 007, the most celebrated emotional cripple of all time.

I'd explained this to Tracy since my return from the funeral. She told me that John Bryce was far more funny, imaginative and loving than 007 could ever be. 'You're enough for me, John. And enough for yourself. James Bond is silly. He isn't real. He's no more real than Noddy.'

I thought of that fateful Valentine message in *The Guardian* that I'd mistaken for an avowal of love from my future wife:

JB, you don't know it,
but you are much loved.

Bond was never truly united with his Bond girls, not in the films or the books. Tiffany Case lived with him in his Chelsea flat after their adventure in *Diamonds Are Forever*, but it didn't work out. Vesper Lynd, the girl from *Casino Royale*, took an overdose before he could tell her that he loved her. His wife Tracy was shot dead by Blofeld at the end of *On Her Majesty's Secret Service*.

In contrast to Bond, I had been given a second chance; a chance not only to be physically present in the lives of my wife and child, but to conquer the strange emotional coldness that had driven me away from them. Whether that coldness set me apart from other men, or acted as a special *bond* that I shared in common with them, I could not say.

On leaving the washroom, I checked Room 4. Tracy had not returned. James was still sleeping. Although I'd decided to trust Shatterheart, I still found it hard to believe that James had a heart complaint. He looked so healthy and strong. I leaned over the cot and kissed him. Then I pressed my nose to his temple, where his natural scent was at its strongest, and breathed him in.

To my immense relief, my boy didn't smell of hospitals or death. He smelled of milk and rusks and Johnson's baby lotion. I leaned closer and whispered in his ear. *'Stay alive,'* I said. Stay alive, so that one day, when you're a giddy seven-year-old playing on the beach, your ageing, disreputable father can point proudly to the scar on your chest and say: *'I think he got the point . . .' (All the dads laugh.)*

I knew where Tracy would be, and decided to go to her. A noticeboard on the wall near the exit caught my eye. It displayed photographs of the staff who worked on the ward, along with their names and job titles. Dr Mervyn was there, looking a few years younger, slightly less ill and grey. Next to him was a photograph of my arch-foe, Mr Emil Shatterheart; not a monster at all, just a small inoffensive boffin with glasses and a neat side-parting.

Glancing down, I saw that 'the brilliant psychopath' wasn't called Shatterheart at all. The title underneath the snapshot read: EMIL CHATTO-HART MD FRCS, CONSULTANT CARDIOTHORACIC SURGEON. I laughed out loud at my own mistake. In my irrational desire to demonise the man who was about to operate on my son, I had rechristened (or antichristened) him with a name more fitting for a Bond villain. In truth, he was nothing but an educated rich boy with a double-barrelled name.

Jesus Christ. I'd been a long way down.

I found Tracy in the hospital chapel, gravely leafing through the book in which parents wrote down their personal messages for God. 'You all right?' I asked her. She turned to me. Her face was white and drawn. There were dark shadows under her eyes. She was coming down with a cold.

She smiled. 'Couldn't sleep to save my bloody life.'

'Me neither.'

'Fuck, some of the stuff in this book is awful,' she said. She turned to a page and read an extract aloud: '"Dear Lord, thank you today for taking our Geoffrey. He has suffered enough but we know you will take care of him in heaven."'

'Don't,' I said. 'I don't want to hear it.'

She ignored me and turned to another page. 'It gets worse. What about this? "Blessed Mother, please send Megan a donor soon." That means: "Please let another child die so that mine can live."'

I shrugged. 'What's surprising about that? It's human nature. We're no different.'

She was silent for a few moments. Her eyes searched mine. 'John. Do you think he's going to be all right?'

It was an unfair question. I took a deep breath. 'Yes,' I said. 'Because whenever something really bad is going to happen, I always dream about it before the event. There haven't been any dreams about James. No feelings of foreboding, nothing. So if you're asking me what I believe, I believe he's going to be fine. But if I'm wrong, I hope you'll still sit next to me at the funeral.'

This made Tracy laugh. She and I had been making sick jokes since my return. Stupid, inane jokes that probably wouldn't seem remotely funny to anyone else, but kept us giggling in the face of despair. One of our favourite jokes concerned how James might grow up to live a useful life despite being a 'heart baby'. For example, he could provide invaluable assistance to a football team. During training, the team could hang him from the cross bar and practise kicking penalties through the hole in his heart.

Tracy reached out and touched my face. There was no mistaking the affection in her eyes. 'Ah. You're lovely.' She put her arms around me and held me. There was a creaking sound behind us, but I didn't look back. 'You're yourself again. You're so nice when you're just being yourself.'

I wasn't feeling 'nice' at all. 'Do you fancy a walk?' I suggested.

'No. I want to go to sleep. I'm so tired, you wouldn't believe it.'

'Actually, I think I would. Believe it, I mean.'

I glanced behind. We were no longer alone. There was a young woman sitting in the last pew. Her hands were clasped and her head was bowed. I suddenly felt out of place. Unlike Tracy, I'd never believed in God. 'Come on. Let's go for a lie-down.'

We went back to the baby's room. James was fast asleep. Tracy and I flopped onto the lumpy camp-bed that so many anxious parents had tossed and turned on before us. And we held on to each other for dear life. In moments, Tracy fell into a blessedly deep slumber. I left her to rest and went downstairs for a smoke.

I walked past the uniformed security man at reception and through the automatic doors. Then I stood under the canopy of the covered walkway, near the PLEASE DO NOT SMOKE sign, watching the rain and sleet lashing down Great Ormond Street. Christ! What a fix!

I grimaced as I reached into my jacket and withdrew one of the strongly flavoured cigarettes that had been specially made for me by Gitane, the cigarette people. Since purchasing these cigarettes in France, I had already managed to smoke ten out of a possible twenty! I drew the bitter healing smoke deep into my lungs. I wanted to be completely fit and relaxed for an operation that might last most of the morning.

A taxi pulled up and the driver put down his passenger; an old man in a wheelchair. Not wishing to be rude, I stared into the middle distance as the invalid wheeled past me towards the hospital entrance. But then he stopped, coughed and said: 'Are you? Are you?'

I had heard that voice so often in my imagination that at first I failed to respond. I continued to stare out at the bleak night. The man in the wheelchair rolled forward to gently nudge my legs with his knees. 'Son?'

I looked down and gasped. There was no mistaking that ruddy sailor's face, the briar pipe dangling from the corner of that thin, rather sour mouth or those damnably clear grey eyes with their look of cold command. 'Dad!' I said as I squeezed his shoulder.

Instantly, I felt him recoil from my touch with that horror of close physical contact that is common to so many Englishmen. 'Are you?' he said with a gasp, as if he was trying to say: *'Are you a homosexual?'*

There was a metallic bleep as the pipe (or Damaged Left Cerebellum Decoding Device) was activated. In seconds, the gadget had neutralised the devastating effects of his stroke and M was free to speak again. In his own voice with its beloved Salford accent he said: 'What the hell d'you think you're playing at?'

I was so excited that my teeth began to chatter. 'Is it you, Dad? Is it really you? But that's amazing. You faked your own death, just like I faked mine in that terrible film they made of *You Only Live Twice.*'

'No. I'm dead all right.' M looked abashed. 'Except I didn't die. I, er, sort of walked into the next room. Or words to that ruddy effect.'

I attempted to embrace him. He forestalled me by displaying the palm of his hand, like a policeman on traffic duty. 'This isn't a social call, 007 . . .'

007? Why the hell was he calling me that? I shook my head emphatically. Almost kindly, M said: 'The double-0 prefix is a great honour. It's brought you the only assignments you know – the heart-breaking ones. You can't run away from your destiny, James.'

It was all happening again, and I was powerless to prevent it. 'Dad?'

'Your orders were to kill Shatterheart. Instead, you spared his life. You're meant to be an assassin, man. What're you trying to do? Win the humanitarian of the year award?'

'It was just a feeling, sir . . . I decided he was just a surgeon, not a criminal mastermind at all . . . and that when you briefed me that night, I was having some kind of hallucination.'

M scowled in derision. 'Then I'll recall 0011 from Cheadle Hulme. He obeys orders, not feelings . . .'

I looked into M's eyes with real resentment. 'I think you . . . we've made a mistake, sir. And his name isn't Shatterheart. It's *Chatto-Hart.*'

The old man's left fist hammered down on the arm of his wheelchair. 'Have you taken leave of your senses, man? *I'll* decide who's made a mistake or not. Either you finish the job, or face the consequences.'

'What consequences? You have no power over me, Dad.'

M tutted and rolled his eyes towards heaven. 'Well, isn't it bloody marvellous?' This was always my father's supreme expression of disgust.

I was trembling violently now. 'Also, we can't be having this conversation because you're dead. And even if you aren't dead, you suffered a major stroke, and all you can say is "are you, are you". And I can't be James Bond because James Bond is a fictional character, invented by Ian Fleming in 1952. My name is John Bryce, the eldest son of Ivy and Myles Bryce. That's you, Dad. You've never been the Head of British Intelligence. You were a signwriter who became the manager of a struggling printing firm.'

M's face turned dark-red. I had never seen him so angry. But I had to tell him the truth. I couldn't stop myself. 'This James Bond fixation of mine is an escape I invented as a kid, because I felt reality was too unpleasant. I thought Mum was Rosa Klebb, for God's sake!'

'You blithering young fool!' exploded M. 'Don't you realise what Shatterheart's done? The blasted man's *de-programmed* you.'

'Sir?'

The cold eyes blazed. 'And stop saying "sir". You sound like a ruddy scullery maid! I don't know how they did it, but the other side have brainwashed you, just as you were brainwashed by the KGB before the opening scene of *The Man With The Golden Gun*.'

I was upset, but not too upset to be anal. 'I take it you're referring to the book, not the dreadful film?'

'Actually, the book was pretty dreadful too,' mused M. 'Not Fleming's fault. Poor devil couldn't help dying before he'd finished it . . .' M waved his pipe irritably, annoyed by his own digression. 'I'm not here to discuss cheap fiction, dammit! You used to be one of my best agents. Now it appears you've gone soft. Suppose I'll have to buy you a frock and put you in the typing pool.'

Anger surged through me. The cold-hearted old bastard! 'If that's your attitude, sir, then you have my resignation.'

M humphed sarcastically. 'You just told me you didn't work for me. How can you resign from a job you've never had?' (He had me there. I was shocked into silence.) 'Now stop shouting and calm down. I'm not really going to make you wear a frock. I was joking.'

Mollified, I said: 'Sorry, sir. You're not known for your sense of humour . . . not in the films or the books or real life, for that matter . . . in fact, the only time you ever seemed happy was at the outset of a family holiday, before the boredom set in. Or when you came in mildly pissed after a night out with Auntie Edna and Uncle Vernon. Or when you were watching the Morecambe and Wise Christmas show . . .'

'As I've explained, I'm not acting in the capacity of father, 007,' M reminded me sternly. 'I'm here as your superior. The fact remains that Shatterheart's still alive because you were damn' fool enough to let him hoodwink you.' M sighed, in awe of my stupidity. '*Chatto-Hart*, my eye! I suppose you'll be telling me next that I'm Dame Judi Dench!' (As I said, wit had never been M's strong suit.) He sucked on the pipe and drew in a deep lungful of smoke. 'Anyway, this is now an emergency. Crash-dive and ultra-hush. Something has to be done.'

'But surely you don't expect me to get at Shatterheart here? Not with all his people around him?'

M sucked on his pipe ruminatively. His eyes mellowed. 'No. Far too late for that. Just tell me about my grandson. Does he seem ill to you?'

I blew out a cloud of cigarette smoke resignedly. 'No sir. He looks the very picture of health. But then, I'm no doctor . . .'

'Precisely. You only kill professionals. Doctors kill anyone they can get their hands on.' M stuck his pipe in his mouth and laid each of his hands flat on the arms of his wheelchair. It was the old familiar gesture that he always made when he came to the sixty-four-dollar question, or when he was about to tell me off for a bad school report.

'Now, for the last time, *there is nothing wrong with my grandson's heart*. If you can't get Shatterheart away from the baby, then you must get the baby away from Shatterheart. Understood?'

I tensed my jaw. 'His mother won't like it, sir.'

'What's Shatterheart's mother got to do with it?'

'I was referring to Tracy.'

M smiled frostily. 'She'd like the alternative even less. Ever been to a baby's funeral, 007?'

I shook my head.

'Ghastly business,' said M. 'Everyone crying. Tiny little coffin, no longer than your arm. That what you want, is it?'

'No sir,' I answered firmly. 'It is not.'

'Then . . . are you . . . you . . . you know what to do.'

I nodded, pretending not to notice M's faltering speech. The DLCDD concealed in his pipe was running low on power. 'Yes, sir.'

He extended his good hand to me. I shook it warmly.

'Good luck,' said M. 'Are you, are you.'

A lump came to my throat. Then I turned my back on the greatest spymaster the world had ever known. As I walked away, he spoke again. 'And son . . .' I halted, without looking back. 'Son . . . are you . . . are you.' (He was really struggling now.) 'In answer to that question you . . . are you . . . asked me a while ago . . . I are you. I . . . are you . . . with all my heart.'

I spun around, but there was absolutely no one there. The wind moaned softly as I ran to the end of the walkway and looked both ways. But M had vanished and I saw only the drab London night and the black relentless rain lashing down Great Ormond Street.

12

To Guard A Living Target

I re-entered the hospital and took the lift up to the fifth floor. A black orderly was mopping the floor outside the lift doors. His strong, high-cheekboned face seemed strangely familiar. A warm wave of delight washed over me when I realised where I had seen that face before. I held my forearm over my eyes in the traditional salute of the Cayman Islanders.

'Hello, Quarrel!' I said. I had been under the impression that my old friend perished on Dr No's island. Remembering the way that Quarrel had spoken in both *Live And Let Die* and *Dr No*, I said: 'Dis is really someting, ol' fren'. I sho never did tink I was goin' to see yo face again . . .'

Quarrel blinked uncertainly. 'Is something wrong, Captain?'

'Well, what meks yo ask that, mon?' I said, startled by his sagacity.

He said: 'Well, I don't mean to be personal, but you appear to be performing the most ridiculous parody of a West Indian patois that I've ever heard.'

I shrugged. 'Something else that Fleming got wrong?'

He grinned, showing less pearly white teeth than I remembered. He had aged considerably since our last meeting. 'I'm afraid so. Fleming's attitude to black Jamaicans was well intentioned but dreadfully patronising. In that respect, he was very much a product of his time. I may have been a poor fisherman, but he chose to overlook the fact that I also earned a 2.1 in Philosophy at Kingston University.'

'You've got a degree?' I marvelled. 'So how come you're mopping floors?'

'For the same reason that I was forced to eke out a living as a fisherman. The modern world doesn't have much use for philosophers.'

'I'm sorry, Quarrel,' I said with feeling. 'I thought you were just a plucky but servile black stereotype.'

He smiled ruefully. 'The story of my life.' Pausing, he peered into my face with concern. 'Excuse me, Captain . . . but are you in some kind of trouble?'

'What makes you say that?'

'Well, the lines under your eyes and on your forehead suggest that you've experienced a great deal of pain and stress since our last meeting. And if you'll forgive me, you appear to be crying.'

'I'm not crying.' I retorted. 'I've got something in my eye.' I saw the silent compassion in his face and was touched by it. Good Cayman Islanders make the finest, most loyal servants in the world. 'I'm afraid it's bad, Quarrel. I'm in trouble. You've never met Tracy, but she's a wonderful girl. One of the most wonderful girls I've ever known. Well, we've had a baby and it's perfectly healthy, but they're trying to kill it. I've got to get it away.'

Quarrel nodded sympathetically. 'I knew something was wrong. Is there anything, anything at all, that I can do to help?'

'As a matter of fact, there is. The kid's in Room 4. My wife's in there asleep. Would you go in and see if anyone's around? And if there isn't, would you smuggle the baby out to me? For God's sake, don't wake up Tracy. She mustn't find out what we're up to . . .'

'Sure thing.' Quarrel beamed. 'Or should I say "Sho ting"?' He laughed exuberantly. This was just the sort of excitement he'd been hoping for when he got a job as a hospital cleaner.

He passed through the swing doors, leaving his mop and his bucket behind. After about a minute, the swing doors opened. My heart almost stopped when a nurse walked through and headed straight for me. But she merely gave me a bland smile, pressed the 'down' button and waited for the lift. When it arrived, she entered and the metal doors closed behind her.

Seconds later, Quarrel returned. He was perspiring and out of breath. There was a rolled-up towel tucked underneath his left arm.

I said: 'You didn't disturb Tracy?'

Quarrel grinned happily. 'No. She's sleeping like the proverbial log.'

He lifted a corner of the towel to reveal a small head covered in damp, dark curls. Miraculously, James was still asleep. 'Wasn't there a carry cot?' I asked him.

Quarrel's face dropped. 'Oh, Lord. I didn't think to look. Would you like me to go back for it?'

'No, Quarrel. You've done enough.'

I reached into my pocket, pulled out a twenty-pound note and tried to press it into his palm. But he pushed my hand away sternly. 'Please. Don't treat me like a "nigger-for-hire". I'm your *friend*, for God's sake.'

I said nothing, but a lump came to my throat. Already regretting his outburst, Quarrel gently handed over the bundle. He gazed at the sleeping child and smiled. 'Captain, he really is a beautiful boy. You must be very proud of him.'

'Yes,' I answered uncertainly. 'I suppose I must.'

'Take good care of him. And of yourself. Do you hear?'

'I hear you loud and clear, Quarrel.'

His brow furrowed with perplexity. 'As your friend, I have to ask you: Are you sure you know what you're doing?'

'Let's just say I'm acting on the strictest orders.'

Quarrel slapped my shoulder. 'Not that it matters. I haven't had so much fun since *Dr No*.'

I hugged him, then headed for the stairs.

Before reaching the ground floor, I took off my jacket and wrapped it carefully around my son. I tucked the resulting bundle under my arm, aware that it looked ludicrously suspicious. Then I crossed the brightly lit entrance hall, fully expecting to bump into Shatterheart on the way out.

But I met no one, and the solitary guard on reception was in the middle of a phone call. He didn't look up as I walked past him. The automatic doors whisked open. With exhilaration born of hope and fear, I stepped out into the rain and ran to the side street where the DB7 was parked.

As I unlocked the car, the glow of a streetlamp fell on James's carry cot, already strapped to the back seat. I was confused, and then alarmed when a dark shape stirred inside the car. I opened the door and the interior light flashed on. A small neat man with sandy hair was sitting in the front passenger seat. He was wearing an enormous chunky cardigan that his wife must have knitted for him. I recognised him immediately as Major Boothroyd, the Head of Q Branch.

'Late as usual,' he said with more than a hint of disapproval.

I laughed in surprise. 'Q! What the hell are you doing here?'

Major Boothroyd and I had never really seen eye to eye, not since *Dr No* when he said my faithful Beretta belonged in a lady's handbag. But tonight, I was more than happy to see him.

I sat beside him with the baby in my lap. Then Q held out his hand. 'I don't know whether you're aware of this, 007, but as a government agent, you're not authorised to carry pretend guns. So I must ask you to hand over your Walther PPK.'

'I've lost it. I think it's still in the wardrobe at that hotel in Deauville. It was useless anyway. Kept falling out of its bloody holster.'

Q nodded sagely. 'For once, this abuse of government property wasn't your fault. You were suffering from one of Ian Fleming's technical bloopers, I'm afraid. Although he gives you a Berns Martin Triple-Draw holster for your Walther in *Dr No*, this holster is really only suitable for revolvers. Fleming knew next to nothing about guns.'

'But he knew a little about women.'

'Really?'

'No. He knew even less about women than he knew about

guns. Which is still a hell of a lot more than your wife knows about knitting.'

'Oh, be quiet, can't you?' Q snatched the sleeping baby off me and rocked it gently. He said: 'Now on to more important matters. Someone's got to teach you how to look after this little fellow. Unfortunately, the job's fallen to me.' His clear, cold, wide-apart grey eyes softened slightly as he surveyed James's face. Then he eyed me with considerably less warmth. 'Now pay attention, 007. This is a three-month-old baby. Sleeps for approximately four hours at a time. Drinks Cow & Gate Premium, heated to body temperature.

'The front end fires a stream of hot urine at a moment's notice. Range: four to five feet. The back end emits noxious gases and missiles of faecal matter.'

I laughed. 'Faecal matter? You're joking!'

Q eyed me coldly. 'I *never* joke about my work, 007. This baby has spent nine months gestating in the womb. Already, it's genetically programmed to turn into a fully active human being, complete with emotions, needs and idiosyncratic mental and physical attributes. It's a living miracle and for once, we'd like it back in one piece, along with your other equipment, on your return from the field.'

'Oh.' I smirked, in my finest Sean Connery accent. 'You'd be shurprised at the amount of wear and tear that goesh on out there in the field.'

As a boy, watching the Bond films at the cinema, I always thought of Ashleigh field when I heard Q refer to 'the field'. Ashleigh field was a small park in Hazel Grove, where I was born. Once, in Ashleigh field, I hit a council estate kid for laughing at me. He was bigger than me, but he went home and fetched his dad. His dad, who was six feet tall, came to the park and slapped me across the face so violently that I fell over. So yes, you'd be surprised at the amount of wear and tear that goes on in the field.

Next, Q laid a black leather attaché case on his knees, taking care to turn the locks lengthways before opening them. Had he failed to do this, a canister of CS gas would probably have exploded in his face. He reached into the case and held up an oblong of white material.

'This is a disposable nappy. Any fool can change one of these – even you should manage it. Holds together with these adhesive tabs. See? When they're dirty, you just throw them away.'

'Ingenious.'

Boothroyd's lips tightened. 'Not good for the environment, of course. But nor are most of the things we make at Q Branch.' He held up a smaller packet and a round grey tub. 'Baby-wipes to clean him up. When he's clean, dab each of his firing cylinders with Sudocrem . . . useful for the prevention of nappy rash.

'Finally, wrap the rubbish in one of these easy-seal bags and deposit the whole stinking mess into the nearest bin.'

'Seems rather a harsh way to treat a baby . . .'

The Major was not amused. 'Oh, spare me the frivolity, 007!'

'What'll I do when the supplies run out?'

Q's eyebrows disappeared into his hairline. 'For heaven's sake! Go to a chemist!'

'I only asked.'

Q held up a wad of muslin squares. 'You'll also need these. Particularly useful for mopping up vomit . . .'

I said seriously: 'I usually just lean out of the window.'

Q groaned. '007, at this hour of the morning, I'd be grateful if you'd keep your juvenile quips to yourself.'

'Fair enough.'

'Other miscellaneous items include Calpol, in case he comes down with a temperature, disposable thermometers, assorted vests and baby-grows, cardigans, gripe water, infacol, baby lotion, baby shampoo, towels, dummies, Q tips and lastly, a rattle.'

'What? No radioactive lint?'

Sighing, he held up a baby's milk bottle. 'Also, a good supply of these things. There's a sterilising unit in the boot, along with full instructions. The milk's the most important item . . . once again, you've got a week's supply.'

Q snapped the attaché case shut with one hand, and pushed it over to me. Then he handed me the baby, who whined briefly, kicked his legs and went back to sleep. 'Oh. Nearly forgot.' Q reached into the pocket of his cardigan and withdrew a small teddy bear. 'This is for the little chap. It may look like an ordinary soft toy, but press its tummy and . . .'

'It explodes?'

Q smiled. 'Not quite.' He prodded the bear's midriff. From its depths, a low, growling voice said: 'Daddy.'

Boothroyd's clear eyes narrowed in warmth. He thrust the bear into my free hand. 'Good luck, Commander.'

Then Q slipped out into the night, slamming the car door behind him. With a curt little wave, he turned and walked off towards Russell Square, leaving me alone with the baby and a mounting sense of indescribable dread.

13

All The Time In The World

Once I was out of the city, I headed north-west on the deserted M1, keeping to the middle lane while rain and sleet bombarded the windscreen. In the faint glow of the dashlight, my face was tense and hard. Every few moments, I glanced in the rear-view mirror, ever watchful for the blazing headlights and flashing lights of the police patrol car that for James and me would signify the failure of our mission. But although I overtook a few lorries and dawdling cars, nothing passed me, and the car's mirrors displayed nothing but black emptiness, stretching miles behind me.

For the first hour of the journey, James lay awake in his cot, sometimes gurgling, occasionally breaking wind, but never once crying. He was too young to miss his mother. That honour was left to me. Every few miles or so, Tracy's face would drift into my mind. The thought of the pain she would suffer when she awoke to find me and the baby gone made me feel physically ill. I tried to tell myself that I was a secret agent, a blunt instrument to be wielded by my government during moments of national insecurity. But all I felt was a conflicting sense of guilt, confusion and loss.

M had assured me that I was the real James Bond. Quarrel and Q had clearly been in no doubt that I was the most famous double-0 operative in history. ('Double the danger! Double the women! Double the excitement!') I certainly didn't feel like Bond, but this may have been due to the amnesia I suffered at the end of *You Only Live Twice*. Whoever I was, I had a job to do, a child's life to save. This was no time for vacillation.

I was heading for Stockport. I don't know why. It was only an ugly sprawling town in the north-west of England with a nice shopping centre and a useless football team. I'd grown up near Stockport, kissed my first girl in the shadows of Stockport precinct on a Saturday night, felt her splendid breasts tautening under her Marks & Spencer bra. I liked Stockport, I liked its people. And I had nowhere else to go.

By the time I reached Watford, it was getting on for six a.m. and I no longer had the motorway to myself. I was feeling weak and light-headed. I decided to stop at a service station for a rest and something to eat. The baby, thankfully, had gone back to sleep. Holding his carry cot in one hand and the case from Q Branch in the other, I crossed the car park in the pissing rain. I walked into the restaurant and ordered breakfast.

The man behind the counter was bored and middle-aged, with a neatly trimmed moustache and the obscenely blotchy complexion that one associates with heart disease. His overall and white chef's hat made him look absurd as well as terminally ill. Moodily preoccupied, he took my order without so much as a glance at me.

'Scrambled eggs on wholewheat toast, a large carafe of freshly squeezed orange juice, and a double helping of coffee.'

Abruptly, the man looked up. His face broke into a charming smile and his eyes twinkled. 'Monsieur Bond?'

With a severe inner jolt, I recognised the stranger as my old friend Monsieur Bécaud, the one-time owner of my favourite restaurant in France. No wonder I hadn't been able to locate him during my recent sojourn in Étaples. He was managing a greasy cafe on the M1!

'My dear Bécaud!' I said. 'Is it really you?'

'Mais oui.' He shrugged forlornly. 'Times are hard, Monsieur. We must all do what we can to get by . . .' His face suddenly brightened. 'But I forget my manners. You will be requiring your usual table?'

As far as I knew, I'd never visited this establishment before in my life. But not wanting to hurt Bécaud's feelings, I said: 'If possible, Monsieur.'

'Mais mon cher Monsieur Bond . . . for you, *anything* is possible.' He bent down to give my sleeping son's hand an affectionate pat. This gesture was the man's sole acknowledgement of the embarrassing fact that 007, the notorious seducer and womaniser, had turned up at his establishment with a three-month-old baby in tow. Such exquisite *savoir-faire* had once made François Bécaud the finest restaurateur in France.

He ushered me to a table for two overlooking the motorway. There were dirty cups and plates on the table, and smears of tomato sauce across its surface. Bécaud stacked the dishes onto a tray and gave the table a cursory wipe with a damp, dirty cloth.

Then he drew back a chair for me and with an obsequious bow said: 'Your table awaits.'

I sat down and smoked distractedly for a few moments. Then Bécaud returned with the food. I ate slowly and with absorption. James awoke while I was on my second cup of coffee. He made no sound, merely blinked and gazed serenely about him. Gently, I lifted him out of the cot and slipped him into my left arm. With my free hand, I carefully opened my attaché case, having no desire to spray tear gas into my face. Then I extracted Q's teddy bear and passed it to the baby. He slipped its ear into his mouth and began to suck.

There was a family sitting at the next table: a young couple and their gargantuan baby. The baby was dressed in a silver shell suit. Its father was a thin man with sharp cheekbones and an aura of impending imprisonment. He was reading *The Sun* and eating with his mouth open: two sure indications of his working-class origins. The child's mother looked younger than the man; less tired and careworn. Her face was pretty and good natured. Her shoulder-length hair was council-estate blonde; an unearthly shade of greenish yellow. Yet in spite of her oafish husband, gross baby and badly dyed hair, she emanated quiet contentment. I liked her on sight.

The baby was lying across her lap, kicking its portly legs in the air while its mother poured formula milk down its eager throat. Her husband scowled and concealed himself behind *The Sun*. Its headline read: SEX SWAP SHOCK OF RANDY MANDY. Suddenly the woman said: 'That's a beautiful baby yer've got there.'

'I agree,' I smiled. 'But I'm a little biased.'

I knew that I was taking an unnecessary risk by answering her. When my face was plastered over every newspaper in the country, she would probably remember me. For the time being, I was glad of someone to talk to.

'She's gorgeous,' the woman assured me.

'Actually, it's a boy.'

She gave a nervous little laugh. 'Oh. Sorry.'

'Don't be.' I smiled, glancing down at the small child in my arms and realising that the woman didn't see me as a cold and ruthless spy, but the kind of sensitive, caring father who can never do enough for his children. Suddenly, it was a role that held enormous appeal for me.

'Yeah,' said the woman. 'You can't tell the difference at that age.'

Abruptly, her husband yawned, stretched and stood up. Then, with studied indifference, he slowly ambled away, occasionally tapping his thigh with the rolled-up copy of *The Sun*. His wife smiled shyly. 'Looks like we're off.'

She picked up her bag and the monster baby, which she was somehow still managing to feed. As she passed my table, she paused to gaze at James affectionately.

'Lovely, though, i'nt he? Lovely little lad. 'Ow old is he?'

'Just over three months.'

She looked worried. 'Oh no, pet, 'e must be younger than that. Our Ryan's three months.'

My face started to burn as I studied the fat, pink infant who she was cradling in her right arm. Then I looked down at my own baby. He was almost half the size of 'our Ryan'. For the first time, I saw James's thin, starved arms and legs, the dimness of his eyes, the blueish tinge to his ivory-pale skin. I saw his chest rising and falling with alarming rapidity, the pulse at his tiny throat tugging as he breathed. His forehead was damp. His dark hair was so wet that it was plastered to his scalp. He was sweating because of the sheer effort it cost him to breathe, to stay alive.

My son was desperately ill.

Dazedly, I looked up. The woman was gazing down at me with genuine concern. 'Love? Are you all right, love?'

'Yes,' I said. I held the baby close to me, shielding him with my body as if everything in the universe posed an immediate threat to him. 'He's quite all right, really. He's in no hurry to grow up. You see . . . he's got all the time in the world.'

Mystified and troubled, she followed her husband out of the restaurant. I stared down at James, feeling the woman's eyes upon me as she glanced anxiously back at the strange grey-faced father who didn't know how old his son was. I waited until she had gone, then carried James out, leaving the black attaché case behind. I had no further use for it.

I remained in the fast lane all the way back to London, driving at one hundred and fifty miles an hour. If the police had taken an interest in my speed and flagged me down, I would have simply told the truth. 'My son is dying, Officer. I'm taking him to hospital.' All policemen love children. They would have given me a full escort, sirens blaring. But no other car came near me.

As I drove M suddenly appeared beside me and began to berate me for my change of heart. '007, you have deliberately disobeyed an order. I have no choice but to suspend you from active duty. As of now, your licence to kill is revoked . . .'

Casually, without meeting the old man's eyes, I reached down and flicked open the top of the gear stick, exposing a small red button. 'I mean, what's come over you?' M was saying. 'Are you mad? Well, are you? Are you? Are you?'

I hesitated for a moment. After all, he was my father. I loved him dearly. But the baby came first. And as long as I needed my daddy, I could never be a daddy in my own right. Decisively, I pressed the red button. A split-second later, the roof slid open and M and the seat containing him were rocketed into space. 'Are yooooooo!' he cried, his voice trailing away into the distance.

At that instant, the mobile phone rang. It was Moneypenny, asking to speak to M. 'He's just popped out.' I told her. *(All the dads laugh.)*

Miraculously, I arrived at Great Ormond Street at seven fifteen. Tracy had just awoken, and was asking a nurse where we'd got to as I carried James into the Bonham Carter ward.

'Where've you two been?' Tracy was smiling. There was no trace of panic in her face and manner. She was merely curious. I was in the clear. Had my son not been about to face a life-threatening operation, I might have felt relieved.

There was a hint of reproof in the nurse's voice as she said: 'Not where they should be.'

'What's eating her?' I asked Tracy as we walked back to Room 4.

'Oh, they just came up to give James his pre-med, and neither of you were around, so they got a bit edgy. That's all.'

'I was just taking him for a walk.'

'I know,' she said gently. 'You were trying to memorise him, weren't you?' I passed the baby to her without answering. I didn't know what she was talking about. Tracy's eyes shone as she looked at me. 'In case something goes wrong. You were committing him to memory, weren't you?'

I nodded slowly. Anything was preferable to the truth.

'I did the same thing last night,' she confessed solemnly. Then she kissed James on the cheek. He opened his eyes slowly, not looking at anything in particular. 'Every eyelash, every hair on his head. You know . . . just in case.'

Before I had time to reassure her, two nurses arrived. One restrained James while the other squirted some foul-smelling liquid down his throat. The baby screamed and cried in real distress, then calmed down as the pre-med took hold. The nurses left the room, and Tracy went to the Ladies. For a few moments I was left alone with my son. I slipped my little finger into his right hand. He gripped the finger in his fist as his eyelids grew heavy. I felt a sudden change in the room's atmosphere, turned my head and saw Emil Chatto-Hart standing in the doorway.

(Had he been playing by the rules, this would have been the surgeon's cue to explain the plot and have a good gloat. 'You amuse me, Mr Bond. You have failed in your mission, and you will die a painful and ignominious death. But first, join me in a little television viewing. The Nemesis satellite will soon be activated. In less than a minute, you will watch helplessly as your native Stockport is wiped off the face of the Earth . . .'

'But why?'

At this point, Shatterheart would throw back his head and laugh mockingly. 'Such a hilarious question, Mr Bond. Why does anything cease to exist? However, for the sake of politeness, I will endeavour to answer you. My primary goal is to destroy the morale of the British people by turning their health service into a murder machine. Those who fall ill will never get better! What simpler way to bring a nation to its knees?

'My secondary objective has been to undermine British Intelligence by breaking the heart of James Bond, its greatest agent. I see by your face that my "treatment" is already taking effect.'

Then I would say: 'Shatterheart by name – Shatterheart by nature.'

Shatterheart's attention would then be attracted by a steady bleeping sound, signalling that the Nemesis death ray was now fully engaged and aimed at Stockport. Then some Oriental scientist, preferably played by Burt Kwouk, would commence the countdown. 'Ten seconds and counting . . . nine . . . eight . . .'

Now, where did I hide that exploding cigarette?)

'Mr Bryce?' said Chatto-Hart pleasantly. 'I just want to check that you're quite clear about what we're going to do this morning.'

I'd expected him to be dressed for surgery in a green cap and smock, but he was wearing a dapper brown herringbone sports jacket and neatly pressed fawn trousers. His hair, as always, was neatly parted to the left and the sharp eyes glittered watchfully behind the thick lenses of his spectacles.

'Yes,' I replied evenly as he walked towards me. 'You're going to patch up the hole between the upper chambers of James's heart. But your main worry is that the left side of his heart is small compared to the right, and won't be able to cope with the increased flow of blood.

'And if that proves to be the case, you'll know immediately because his heart won't beat when you take him off bypass.'

Chatto-Hart nodded. I could see that he was impressed. 'Yes. That's right on the button.' He smiled. 'You look a lot better, Mr Bryce. Are you feeling it?'

Nodding, I smiled back at him. 'I just couldn't admit the baby was ill. Couldn't face the truth at all, Doctor.' Then I blushed slightly, remembering that surgeons were always addressed as 'Mister' not 'Doctor'.

Chatto-Hart didn't seem to notice my social blunder. 'Well, I'll be performing your son's operation personally,' he said grandly. 'I'll do my very best for him. I can't promise much, but I can promise you that.'

Then Emil Chatto-Hart laughed. It was the first time I'd ever seen him laugh and the effect was startling. The harsh lines around his eyes and mouth disappeared, transforming the cold and peevish surgeon into a kindly, intelligent little boy.

With this, Chatto-Hart slapped me on the arm and walked briskly away. I never saw him again. Tracy returned from the lavatory, dabbing her eyes. Then three anaesthetists arrived to take the baby away. James was fast asleep, but Tracy still insisted on carrying him down to theatre. I remained beside the empty cot, half-hoping that Q would reappear to equip me with an Anti-Operation-Stinger-Missile so that I could blow the operating theatre apart before James reached it, and a Punctured-Baby-Repair-Kit, enabling me to patch up James's heart in the privacy of my own home.

When Tracy returned, we stood in the centre of Room 4 for a long time, clinging tightly to each other, loving each other without speaking because we had already said all that needed to be said. Then we put on our coats and walked out of the hospital. It was shortly after nine o'clock.

We'd been advised not to stay in the hospital, but to shit bricks elsewhere and return at noon, when the operation would definitely be over. The rain had stopped, and the sun was shining. We could have spent the next few hours sitting somewhere beautiful like Kensington Gardens or St Paul's Cathedral. However, if James didn't make it, we knew that wherever we'd spent his last hours on earth would be for ever tainted by association with his death. So Tracy and I deliberately chose to go somewhere that we would never want to visit again. We went to a McDonald's restaurant in Victoria.

I have no idea what we talked about as we ate our burgers and fries. I know that we made sick jokes and chatted amiably, like two shipwreck survivors mocking the circling sharks. I recall that there was a peculiar 'stagey' quality to our conversation, both of us acting as if James's survival was a foregone conclusion and that the open-heart surgery he was undergoing was little more than an irksome formality, like being inoculated against polio or cutting his first tooth.

Our mood inevitably darkened as noon drew nearer. We continued to make stupid jokes as we travelled underground on the Victoria line to Green Park, then caught a Piccadilly line train to Russell Square. The jokes dried up as we walked through Cosmo Place to Great Ormond Street. We held hands in silence, so afraid that our enjoined palms squelched with sweat. Our stomachs heaved, racked by a debilitating nausea for which McDonald's could not be held responsible. When we came to the hospital entrance, we were almost tempted to walk by, to look the other way, as if we were two tourists out for a stroll and James was someone else's problem.

In the lift up to the fifth floor, I suddenly knew that my son was dead, knew beyond doubt that his small body was already waiting for us in the hospital mortuary. I went cold from head to foot, preparing myself for Tracy's despair, wondering if they'd had the decency to sew my dead boy up, or whether his gaping wound had simply been covered in a makeshift dressing.

Because of my bitter foreknowledge, I was taken aback by the callousness of the sister at reception. She greeted us with an unctuous smile. She was small and dark, with an irritatingly high voice. 'Mr and Mrs Bryce? Yes. Everything's gone well. James is fine. Mr Chatto-Hart is very pleased with him. He's down in CICU and you can see him as soon as you like.'

Tracy and I practically skipped down the stairs to the third floor. As soon as security had cleared us, we entered the cardiac intensive care unit to be at our son's side. He had his own personal nurse. She was sitting on a stool beside him. With his spreadeagled arms and legs, James resembled some beautiful, rare butterfly, cruelly pinned out for our inspection. He was breathing with the aid of a ventilator, his tiny chest rising and falling to the rhythm of its cold, mechanical heart. His vertical chest wound was covered in a neat dressing. Twin drainage tubes, held in place with stitches, had been inserted below the incision to siphon off any excess fluids from his chest. His feet and hands were clad in woollen socks and mittens.

A soft toy lay on a stand above James's head. It was a blue dolphin. The nurse explained that all the children who'd undergone heart bypass surgery were given a blue dolphin as a gift from the hospital. Then I remembered Edward, whose heart bypass surgery had also been scheduled for that morning, and I walked round CICU looking for him. But Edward wasn't there.

Stunned, I returned to my son's side. Quoting Sean Connery in *Goldfinger*, after he has slyly slashed two tyres on Tilly Masterson's white Mustang convertible to send car and driver careering into a ditch, I looked down at James and said: 'You know, you're lucky to be alive.'

Then I started to cry. Not just repressed sniffles, but loud, disgraceful sobs that echoed through the huge room. How odd! How very odd! This hadn't happened to me since I was young. I was heartily glad that M wasn't there to witness my emotional display. In the old navy, men who wept in public were known as 'cry-babies'.

I averted my face and released a harsh expletive. Tactfully, the nurse at James's side passed Tracy a tissue, which Tracy passed to me. I blew my nose and dried my eyes. Then I turned to Tracy. She was smiling. A single tear slid down her cheek. 'At last,' she said, stroking my wet face. 'Thank God for that.'

'This never happened to the other fella,' I quipped.

But Tracy had never seen *On Her Majesty's Secret Service*, so my joke was wasted on her. She held me close and stroked my hair. I felt her magnificent/splendid/fine/faultless breasts tautening under her blouse.

'You've no idea, have you?' she whispered. 'No idea how much you mean to me.' ('**JB**, *you don't know it, but you are much loved.*')

We kept vigil by our child's cot for the remainder of the afternoon, while gleaming machines peep-peeped around us. At five, the cold that Tracy had been fighting finally overwhelmed her and she was obliged to go to bed.

The walk back to our room was marred by a curious incident. Passing through the swing doors to the Variety Club wing, we came face to face with Quarrel, who was busily sweeping the floor. But when I attempted to introduce him to Tracy, my old friend backed away from us, shaking his head. 'You're a mad man,' he said. 'I've already told you. I don't know you. Hear me? I *do not* know you . . .'

While Tracy slept, I returned to my son's side. *My son, my son*. The child who had once been little more than an irritant to me had now become the focal point of my entire life.

The staff had changed shifts. A new nurse was sitting by the baby's cot. She had short dark hair, a warm smile and appallingly loud socks. I commented on the socks, which were covered in tiny images of Tom and Jerry playing cat and mouse.

'Yeah,' she admitted, grinning. 'We have competitions every month to see who can wear the worst pair. The winner gets a bottle of champagne.'

'Bollinger or Dom Pérignon?'

She laughed. 'Safeway. They do a nice bottle at a very affordable price.'

'Just a bottle? Or do they put something in it?'

'Very good. That was almost funny.'

Humour has its own dialect. Something about the nurse's particular brand of sarcasm seemed familiar. 'Good God,' I said. 'You're not from Stockport, by any chance?'

'From Stockport with love,' she confirmed.

'Hey! Don't tell me you're a Bond fan as well!'

'No,' she said. 'Sorry. I used to have a boyfriend who was Bond-mad. I can't stand James Bond.'

The nurse was called Katy. She came from Heaton Moor, a ten-minute drive away from Hazel Grove. She was on duty until ten o'clock that night. I was comforted by her blend of warmth and efficiency and felt that James was in safe hands. So I took a stroll down Great Ormond Street.

I passed a young man who was sitting in a doorway, a sleeping bag over his knees. He asked me for some change. I didn't have any change, so I gave him my cigarettes and my black Ronson lighter. I had a feeling that I wouldn't be needing them any more.

As I walked, a crumpled wad of paper fell out of my jacket onto the road. I picked it up and unravelled it under the light of a street lamp. It was a cheque from the casino in Deauville, to the value of fifty million francs. Not that it was likely to do me much good. The cheque was crossed and made out to 'James Bond 007'.

Yet as I gazed up at the stars, I felt truly blessed. I had a beautiful wife who loved me. I had a child who had suffered a terrible ordeal, but would grow up to be dashing and brave, with a face as brutal and cold as his father's.

I'd been a good agent in my time. But now I had a family. Two people who depended on me. Maybe it was time to abandon all the fast-living and the gunplay, and plan for the future.